TOUGH BLOWS

A Lifelong Journey of Defying the Odds

By Wayne D. Magee

Printed in the United States of America

2018 First Edition

10 9 8 7 6 5 4 3 2 1

Subject Index:

Magee, Wayne D.

Title: Tough Blows: A Lifelong Journey of Defying the Odds

1. Memoir 2. Music 3. Leadership 4. Christian 5. Inspirational

Library of Congress Card Catalog Number: 2018911059

Paperback ISBN: 978-0-692-17917-8

WDM 4:13 LLC

www.toughblows.com

TOUGH Blows Standing Ovation ...

"Wayne Magee is a shining example of one man's triumph over numerous *Tough Blows* since birth. His life is a demonstration that medical science can be inaccurate and he has worked incredibly hard to prove naysayers wrong. I have been fortunate to have a mass amount of talent walk the halls of our music school. Wayne Magee was clearly one of those talented musicians who made my teaching more rewarding."

Dr. Stephen L. Gage, Director of Bands & Orchestra
Youngstown State University Dana School of Music

"At first, I admit, I was apprehensive; the hiring committee was recommending an inexperienced young man from Ohio with no military or apparent leadership experience, who was just barely older than the cadets he would be assigned to command. The Massachusetts Maritime Academy desperately needed someone to lead our growing Band and Honor Guard contingents but was he the right choice? As it turned out, the committee was correct - Wayne Magee turned out to be the best Band and Honor Guard Officer MMA had ever had.

Talented, engaging and incredibly hard-working, Wayne quickly earned the respect of his cadets and everyone in his chain of command. He hustled everywhere he went, he volunteered for every charitable effort, he lived his life with a mixture of humility and genuine concern for everyone in his care. In short, Wayne became an incredibly important and widely respected member of the biggest and best Maritime College in America. I am honored to call him a friend."

RADM Rick Gurnon, USMS (ret.)
Massachusetts Maritime Academy

"One of the greatest teachers in life is a hardship but only the strong, love-filled and wise take the most positive life-altering lessons from it. Ltn. Wayne Magee has been a demonstration of this wisdom, love, and strength. Having read his story in such vivid, perspicuous, emotional yet entertaining manner one has to wonder what excuses are we giving ourselves for remaining bitter and defeated in life. Surely we all have a purpose for being born and we owe it to our Creator to find out and live out that purpose because it is good. Ltn. Magee has given us not only a human relatable example but also very practical tools on how to do just that, this book is nothing short of an awakening. What a gentleman, a champion, what we see when we look at him."

Dr. Portia Ndlovu, Ph.D.
Professor; International Maritime Business

"An inspirational tale of courage, overcoming adversity, and a resolute spirit. Wayne is one of the most humble people I have met in my life...yet, there is a tiger inside. His story is meant for anyone needing some motivation to overcome a personal challenge."

Dr. John F. Korn
Former Dean of Undergraduate Studies at Massachusetts Maritime Academy
Instructor Harvard University, Division of Continuing Education

"As I read the pages of *Tough Blows*, I am overwhelmed by the faithfulness of our Lord. Wayne's testimony inspires and bears witness of the greatness of our Lord and Savior, Jesus Christ. Jesus replied, "What is impossible with man is possible with God" (Luke 18:27). Wayne has been given the title of, "The Last Magee Man." I could not think of anyone better to represent hard work, valor, and strength than the footprints of Wayne. When I want my son to be motivated, I share with him the testimony of Wayne Magee. As a Christian, I sometimes forget to acknowledge my omnipresent Lord. He is there at the beginning and end. He orchestrates His love and compassion like a symphony to direct our path. I am honored to have experienced his workmanship in Wayne's life. I once asked Wayne, "What can I do as a parent to keep my son on the right path?" With boldness and gentleness that only Wayne can project, He answered, "Pray for him and keep him in church."

Pamela R. Belle,
Physical Therapist, Doctor of Physical Therapy

Dedication

This book is dedicated to my mother Ida L. Magee (1927-2015) and my brother Leander E. Magee (1959-2017), whose love and support gave me the means to live a life defying the odds.

Acknowledgments

When I look back on this portion of my life and in preparing this book, I would be remiss not to express my gratitude for the people who have taught me so much through their mentorship, patience and unconditional love, all which has encouraged me to become the man I am today.

Mr. Jerry Allen, thank you for your guidance, shared wisdom, and prayers that have kept me focused.

Mr. Charles Russell, thank you for taking the time to show me the value of hard work and what it looks like to be a Godly man.

Mr. Michael Summers, thank you for your years of dedication and leadership of Liberty Local Schools' music program and the many lives you have influenced for the better through music.

Ms. Lindsay Sullivan, the love of my life, thank you for your love, enduring strength and support. You have taught me more than you will ever know.

Table of Contents

> *"It's not about the cards you're dealt,*
> *but how you play the hand."*
> **-Randy Pausch, The Last Lecture**

Introduction

Proving Them Wrong

"Never allow what they say about you to define you. They said you would not see two years old, that you would be mentally retarded, and with no teeth, you should not be able to blow a trumpet!"

- Ida Magee

But God... The moment that I was able to read and comprehend what was going on inside my body, I realized that my one in one million rare genetic disorder was my opportunity to prove every highly credentialed medical and educational professional unequivocally *wrong*! I was born with cleidocranial dysostosis; *cleido* refers to collarbone, *cranial* means the head, and *dysostosis* is the formation of abnormal bone. This rare disorder affects each person differently, yet the main things we all have in common is that we don't have a collarbone, teeth, and our skull development and facial growth usually appears larger than normal. Neither of my biological parents has my disorder, and there is a 50/50 chance that my children will have it.

Not only did I have physical limitations at birth, but I also had life-threatening respiratory challenges and was often hospitalized. The majority of my doctors provided a negative diagnosis and said that I would not be more than a vegetable and unable to completely develop mentally. Of course, there were the visible complications of my enlarged head, with a big soft spot at the top and my two clavicles were not developed. I have had hundreds of doctor visits and countless surgeries up until I was 18.

I was placed in the Ohio foster care system at four months old and into the home of Ida Magee. She was a deeply religious woman, big in stature and tough, yet with the biggest heart imaginable. At first, she was intimidated by me because I literally had strings attached. There were all types of wires, heart monitors, and equipment connected to me. Not to mention two or three doctors appointments each week.

Throughout my elementary years, I was an introvert. I was just different. Imagine having to wear a white astronaut-like helmet during gym class. I was bullied and teased. The name calling was endless: marshmallow head, heart-head, and E.T., to name a few that were kind. Most of the bullying happened outside of the teachers' earshot, so there was not much I could do. I often came home and told others what happened and many got mad and wanted to retaliate on my behalf. My mother, on the other hand, was of the mindset that I had to stand up for myself. "It's your problem, you handle it. Be a man and handle your own problems and issues," she advised.

My mother, Ida Magee, legally adopted me at 14 years old. The legal battle was arduous because my biological mother was somewhat in the picture, yet she had her own personal challenges to deal with. There were always other foster kids in my home. In 30 years, my mother fostered over 130 kids in the Trumbull County Children's Services Bureau. Even though she only had a second-grade education, she raised all of us to be people of character and respect. Many of my foster siblings are working professionals in medicine, education, politics, and technology fields. Despite growing up in a house full of people, I was very content keeping to myself. I spent more time listening and observing adults than I did speaking. At a young age, I desperately wanted to be an adult and did not waste time doing kid stuff.

I enjoyed every moment being a Boy Scout and envisioned my adult life as a Scout leader. I had no idea that my life's calling would stem from my purchase of a $25 trumpet at a yard sale when I was in sixth grade. It was a family friend's trumpet and it was sitting in their attic for years. They found out that I was interested in learning to play and wanted me to have it for a small fee since the original owner spent about $500 for it. I cleaned it up with a sponge and Dawn Dishwashing Liquid and was instantly hooked! I spent all of my down time learning and practicing knots from the Boy Scout Handbook, playing trumpet and positioning myself within earshot or blending into the woodwork listening to adult conversations.

Nearly two decades later, I am the Director of Bands and Student Leadership Development at a para-military college. I encourage and empower college students each day. My love of music and helping others is what drives me. Looking back, it's as if my life was written as a four-part symphony all along. Each movement in my life was an emotional challenge that required a different thought process and perspective to grow into the next phase.

I am proof that despite many physical setbacks, if you have a big enough *WHY*, no matter how many tough blows or obstacles life sends your way, you can achieve your dreams. By starting with self-leadership, then a keen focus, and determination, all coupled with faith, you can beat any medical or societal odds hands down! For every tough blow, I encourage you to Get T.O.U.G.H!

Be	Tenacious
Seek	Opportunities
Embrace	Unity
Engage	Groups
Ask for	Help

FIRST MOVEMENT

Allegro
Birth - Elementary

Calling all prayer warriors...

CHAPTER 1

Touched By an Angel

"Before I formed you in the womb, I knew you,
Before you were born, I set you apart..."
– Jeremiah 1:5 (NIV)

It's hard to believe that as I write this, I can't help but think about the words the doctors repeatedly told my foster mother at the time, after *every* emergency room visit, "Ms. Magee, he's not going to live past age two, and if he does, he will have severe disabilities." My mentor, Jerry Allen, and others, often told me stories of how at six months old, I was the size of an average man's palm. I was the tiniest human being my mom, or anyone close to her had ever seen. I was connected to a heart monitor 24/7 and I had several tubes and wires coming out of me from every opening. Everyone was afraid to pick me up or gently touch me. The stress of the heart monitor, combined with my biological mother's mental health issues and lack of other family support, was the primary reason I was placed into foster care.

My foster mom was a strong woman of faith. She was steadfast in believing God's Word over the doctor's word. Mom was always praying for the children in her care, the church, her family and extended family. She surrounded herself with people of faith. That's how she connected with my mentor, Mr. Jerry Allen. Mom was friends with Mrs. Vilma Allen from the church. She attended a church banquet and was seated with Mr. and Mrs. Allen. Mr. Allen was a deacon and head of the children's Sunday School. The banquet speaker talked about one of the ten plagues God put on Egypt because Pharaoh refused to let God's people out of bondage. This specific plague was of countless frogs in everyone's home day and night. No one in Egypt could escape them nor have peace from the sounds of "ribbit." They were pests! It was under the plague of the frogs that Pharaoh promised to let the Israelites go, but he later recanted. It was my mother's wit and sense of humor to use the speaker's words to start comedic trouble with those seated around her.

After the speaker took his seat, my mother humorously said to Mr. Allen, "would you be my frog"? Out of respect for her, he responded, "Yes Ma'am," and chuckled. Mom then replied, "sounds like a frog to me!" From that day forward, Mr. Allen and my mom became the best of friends and the "frog warfare" began. They plagued each other with frogs for over 30 years. Frog plush toys, ceramic objects, and greeting cards were all strategically delivered to each other's homes for holidays, birthdays and any other occasion, just to keep the "frog warfare" going. My mother called him "Mr. JD Frog" and he called her "Mrs. Froggie." Together they were a force to be reckoned with as friends fighting spiritual battles in prayer. Their first battle was waged when they teamed up to fight in prayer and support for my survival.

I was described as fragile, tiny and fetal-looking in appearance. Physically handling me was intimidating because the alarms of my heart monitor were always going off. Mr. Allen said that I was the first little baby he had seen hanging in the balance between life and death. He often prayed that I would have a normal life despite my debilitating complications. Even though he was apprehensive, scared and worried about what my mom would say, he came by and picked me up every chance he could. His large hands always got tangled in my wires.

Mr. Allen recalls being there for a visit when my heart stopped. He rode in the ambulance as the paramedics resuscitated me. I was in the hospital for a few days, and the gravity of my condition weighed heavily on my mom and others. When I pulled through, my mom asked Mr. Allen to say a special prayer for me. He wrapped me in a blanket and took me to the corner of the living room, which was off limits for all the other kids in the house. It was a special room in the house for guests. The room that all the kids knew as "the clean room."

He prayed for me like never before. He said that through those wires he sensed and felt a connection between us. It was electric. It was very real for him. He felt that God was speaking to him to be a blessing to me. God answered Mr.

Allen's prayers. In only a few weeks, I started drinking my milk vigorously. I became more alert, stronger and determined to live.

Mr. Allen came by to feed me and pick me up. He felt obligated in his heart and took out time from his own family to play with me, touch me, and do whatever he could because he was still unsure if I was going to make it past my second birthday. His wife Vilma, prayed for me as well. They were a real team. Mr. Allen even attended doctors visits and listened to the negative words they spoke over my life about me potentially being a vegetable and not completely developing. During those early moments, my mom asked him to be my mentor; a God-father of sorts. Out of admiration and respect for her, he agreed. Like my mother, he was always worried about my enlarged head with a big soft spot on top. I also had respiratory problems and was prone to year-round colds. Mr. Allen was by my side as often as he could be. He fixed things around the house and helped out the other kids as well.

Each birthday after my second birthday is truly a blessing from God. It's as if He tapped me on the shoulder and said, "Wayne, I've got you. Keep believing in me and keep reading my Word." I grew stronger with each passing year.

A Hedge of Protection

Before I could walk, I wore a helmet so that I would not injure or irritate my head as it was still developing. I didn't let the helmet stop me. I learned to walk pretty quickly and was very active. My mom wanted to get me off the bottle as soon as possible. One day Mr. Allen came by and she cooked turnip greens and cornbread. She took the pot liquor from the turnip greens and sprinkled the cornbread in a bowl and he fed it to me. In no time, I started growing and began to fit in with some of the other children my age.

I loved the outdoors and my mom had a huge back yard. I roamed around picking up rocks, twigs, leaves and anything interesting I could find. I rode my tricycle full speed and would hit the same turn and fall off. That was my idea of fun. Everyone stood around to watch me hit that turn and fall over and over again. There was always an audience as my mom fostered several children during my childhood and as an adult. I also had Hot Wheels and earth movers that kept me busy. Despite years of respiratory setbacks, chronic ear infections and several ear surgeries, and a host of other problems that stumped the doctors at the Cleveland Clinic and Akron Children's Hospital, my faith grew stronger. My confidence in my abilities increased. I was beginning to feel whole. My two guardian angels, my mom, and Mr. Allen, never gave up on their assignment to nurture me and I began to flourish physically and mentally.

"Have you noticed that as strong as God is, and as powerful as He is, when He speaks, it's with a whisper. The children always listen better when you whisper."
-**Tess**, *Touched by an Angel*

Once I learned to read, I definitely grew wiser. Every-one in our house had to go to church. My mother believed wholeheartedly in God. Whenever I was allowed to be off the heart monitor, I was in church. I loved going to church. It made me feel special, somewhat unique from all the other kids. It was as if God was specifically talking to me in the Scriptures. He knew and understood me like no one else. I soaked up the words of the Bible in my spirit day and night and felt like a grown-up at a young age.

I begged my mother to take me out of the children's church so I could be in regular church with adults who understood the Bible like me. I viewed all of the activities in the children's church were just too playful. I didn't want to play, color, or recite only one or two lines of Scripture. There was this sense of urgency in me. I had no time to play. I was on a special as-signment from God.

CHAPTER 2

A Different World

> *"Tell me and I forget. Teach me and*
> *I remember. Involve me and I learn."*
> **– Benjamin Franklin**

Early on, I was placed in the Fairhaven Program of Trumbull County for children and adults with learning disabilities. I literally rode the little yellow school bus to Fairhaven School. Lunch was provided and I remember there were always a lot of activities involving food like pajama day with movies and popcorn or ice cream sundaes.

The structure of a school was more focused on life skills. I actually found the Fairhaven School more entertaining than challenging. Although my mother was very protective, she instilled life skills to me on a daily basis. So a lot of what they were teaching in school, I was already getting at home. I even took my *McGee & Me*, Christian animated Bible stories on VHS with me to school and was a mini-preacher. I wanted other kids to hear about Christ.

I recall around the first or second grade being moved to the Liberty local public school K-4 grade building. A teacher took me out of my classroom and said, "We're going to get you more help. Come with me." I was escorted out of the regular classroom and put in learning disabilities classes with other kids in my grade. I was given the same class work for the most part but allowed more time to finish. I was also given further academic assistance. The switching classes quickly became boring to me. I could do the work, but I wasn't excited about going because now that I was older, my peers teased me for going to "LD," learning disabilities classes. Not to mention the teasing because of the large white helmet I wore every day at recess or gym class.

My mom always wanted me to be tough. She knew I would face obstacles and she wanted me to be prepared sooner than later. She constantly told me that she was never going to come to school to fight my battles unless I was being abused. A few times she told me that whatever the teacher tells her about me, she will believe the teacher's version over mine.

Around that same time, I liked watching the show "A Different World." One of the main characters, Dwayne Wayne, was played by Kadeem Hardison. I thought his flip-up sunglasses were very cool. He had a similar character name to mine. One day I decided that I wanted to change my name from "Wayne" to "Dwayne." So on of all my exams, seat work, and homework, I wrote "Dwayne," followed by my last name. I did this for what seemed to be a week or two and then one teacher finally confronted me about it. I told her that I wanted to change my name because I liked "Dwayne" better. "Well, I think Wayne is just as nice. So going forward, you will be Wayne in my class," she said.

Thinking back on this seemly harmless decision was my way of coping with having the same first name as my biological father. I knew that he did not want me or even claim that I was his son. He made it clear that he did not want anything to do with a "retarded little baby." Deep down, I wanted to rid myself of his name and take on the name of a black character, who I thought was cool and funny on TV. The next Christmas I begged for those flip-up sunglasses. I got my wish. Needless to say, they did not make it to summer before they broke because of my ill-care of them.

Growing up in Liberty township, a suburb of Youngstown, Ohio, holidays and celebrations were always in full swing. Most of my teachers were Jewish, therefore Jewish holiday traditions were taught in the classroom. I learned to make potato latkes and played with dreidels during Hanukkah. I even went to the bar and bat mitzvah celebrations in my teens.

My least favorite time of year in Youngstown was Halloween. The town went all out to make its events scarier than the year before. I dreaded Halloween every year for 12 years! I just don't like scary things. Everyone on the bus ride to school wore masks and costumes. I rode with my eyes closed. I couldn't even eat lunch that day as I was scared to see something that would upset my eyes and stomach. One time, a couple of kids with devil and monster costumes, cornered me on the bus to force me to look at them. They knew I was scared. I crammed myself between the seats on the bus with my head wedged down. They could not get me to look at them until it was time to get off at school.

Miracle in Ohio

"We are not human beings on a spiritual journey.
We are spiritual beings on a human journey."
– Stephen Covey

As I got older, I didn't mind that my birthday was overlooked since it was so close to Christmas and everyone was in full holiday mode. I was born on December 20th. It's no coincidence that the foundation of my life has been shaped by the Scriptures and the real reason for the holiday season. I really liked the idea of being treated like an adult at only eight years old and was more than happy to take on household chores. On my birthdays, we made homemade German chocolate cake, pound cake with sugar frosting or a 7-up cake.

By this time, my adoptive mother was in her late 60s, so I helped make the cake. She instructed me to bring everything she needed to the kitchen table: blender, butter, eggs, flour, sugar, lemon extract, and her beloved, vanilla extract. She sat at the table and put everything together. My job was to put the cake in the oven and set the timer. She kept a watchful eye on it and did not leave the kitchen until it was done.

I have always been a workhorse. I enjoyed doing anything to help make my mother's day easier, including house cleaning, laundry, and even balancing her checkbook. I also did yard work and took care of things around the house that I learned how to do from Mr. Allen. I was the head bottle washer in the house and became the lead instructor to the new kids that came in the house. For nearly 15 years, I was the top sous chef in the house. I helped plan, prep and prepare all the meals from the age of eight until I left home to move to Massachusetts at 23. I mastered southern and Italian cuisine and still enjoy cooking for others.

Scouts' Honor

"On my honor, I will do my best to do my duty to God and my country..."
- BSA Scout Oath

After two years of Cub Scouts, I joined the Boy Scouts at age 11. I wanted to do everything perfectly. Anything involving rope work, I was determined to master better than anyone in my entire troop. I studied and memorized the Scout Handbook and earned merit badges to advance each year. I was totally all in. Knots were something I became well known for in my troop because I was exceptional at it; the square knot, the granny knot, the slip knot and the bowline knot, which is a life-saving knot that I could actually tie with one hand. One of the Assistant Scout Masters' who was the township's Fire

Chief, challenged me to a duel nearly every time he saw me. It was a duel to see who could tie the bowline knot the fastest. Armed with his rope and both of us at the ready, on the count of three, the battle was on. I often won. Sometimes he beat me. I studied land and celestial navigation, swimming, CPR and first aid. It took anywhere from six months to a year to move up to another rank, and my aggressiveness to advance to the next badge was a constant goal. I am proud to say that I am honored to be an Eagle Scout and I take my oath seriously. Each day I try to live out the core Scouting values. The rank of "Eagle" is a lifelong commitment to self-leadership, as well as leadership in the family, community and the world.

The Great Escape

"Our greatest weakness is giving up. The most certain way to succeed is to try just one more time."
– Thomas A. Edison

I did everything I could to prove to the teachers and administrators that I did not belong in learning disabilities classes for the rest of my life. I created extra credit assignments in math, reading, and science each week. I studied the dictionary and wrote down as many *big* words as I could and begged the teachers to test me on their meaning. I remember seeing Mary Poppins for the first time. I was so impressed by the vocabulary words. I submitted a spelling test to my teachers from the words used in the movie. The first word on my list was "supercalifragilisticexpialidocious." I created tests for every subject. More often than not, I passed with flying colors. My mother and I fought tooth and nail to get me out of the program year-after-year. I was finally helmet free and released from learning disabilities classes in the eighth grade. Onward!

CHAPTER 3

A Date with Destiny

*"For we are His workmanship, created in Christ Jesus
for good works, which God prepared beforehand
so that we would walk in them."*
- ***Ephesians 2:10*** *(NKJV)*

When you look back at where you've been, you will often see the path that led you to where you currently are. My very first date with a girl was at the age of 11, which was just a few months after picking up the trumpet. I got dressed up in my previous Easter Sunday best; a grey suit, white shirt, and black shoes. I escorted a radiant, light-complexioned girl named Laura. My mother and her mother were friends and they arranged for our date to the orchestra. Laura wore a simple yellow dress with a black coat and her hair curled. We were what you call these days, "tweens."

We both looked like a young upper-class couple going out on the town. We went to see the Youngstown Symphony Orchestra at Powers Auditorium in downtown Youngstown. I felt a hundred feet tall. Here I was dressed to impress, escorting a beautiful lady on my arm. She never touched a door. I opened every door for her and made sure she wanted for nothing.

My mother was our chauffeur. She dropped us off in front of the auditorium in her full-size burgundy 1993 Chevy Caprice Station Wagon. For that evening it was our limousine and Laura was my queen. The tickets were acquired via donations from the symphony to the Department of Children and Family Services. I guess not too many families in the system jumped at the chance to see the symphony. But my mother knew that I just started playing the trumpet and thought it would be nice for me to see how my instrument fit into an entire orchestra.

However, what she did not foresee was that in six short years, I would be on that same stage with the Youngstown State University - Dana School of Music Symphony Orchestra, which is the oldest college Orchestra in America. What my mother did not realize is that not only did my date to the orchestra inspire me to continue playing my instrument, but to continue doing what was an anomaly, one black clarinet player on stage. There was also one extremely talented white female percussionist. What I saw in the orchestra was not my experience in life. For the first time, I saw a lack of diversity. I was fortunate to live and go to church in a community of great diversity on every level.

Seeing the orchestra that night with a beautiful curly-haired Laura was the start for me to be the change in the industry that I wanted to see and work in. That night was not just my first date with the gentle Laura, but it was my date with destiny! Some of the musicians in the orchestra that night were people that became my music teachers and mentors only a couple of years later.

CHAPTER 4

Ida the Great
(January 30, 1927 - August 23, 2015)

> *"In the same way, let your light shine*
> *before others, that they may see your good*
> *deeds and glorify your Father in heaven."*
> *– Matthew 5:16 (NIV)*

My mother, Ida Lee Magee was the most God-fearing person I have ever met. She dedicated her life caring for and raising children who were considered the least likely to succeed in Trumbull County. Mom took in all of the kids who were abused or had tragic backgrounds. She was not selective. Yet, she had her work cut out for her with me because she had never taken in an infant with severe medical problems. She was a kind, loving soul, with a heart of gold. She even helped raise her nephew, his children and over 130 kids in Ohio.

Every child who came into her home went to church. We attended Emmanuel Community Church in Austintown, Ohio, on Wednesday nights and Sunday mornings. Regardless of rain, snow or freezing weather, she was there. Mom was an authentic Christian and attended churches under Kathryn Kuhlman's healing ministry. She always arrived early because she was head of the church's daycare. I cannot imagine those brutal Ohio winters when my mother had to get three young kids ready for church, plus me, her "miracle child" with my heart monitor and wires. She also adopted my two sisters, Charmaine and Courtnei.

As long as I can remember, I grew up believing and accepting God. Most of the kids at home hated going to church. I loved it. Especially as I got older and was more involved in the music ministry and played the trumpet. Once my mother allowed me to attend the adult service, I began to challenge the pastor on the sermons he preached. I wanted him to explain certain things to me because I could not reconcile them in my young mind. My mother encouraged me to keep asking questions.

One Sunday, right after church, I cornered Pastor Craig in the hallway and asked, "Did Judas have a choice in betraying Jesus?" I felt that the way it was described in the text, it was as if Judas did not have a choice. Pastor Craig stated, "We all have a choice and he didn't have to do it!" He went on to say that Judas' choice was not taken from him, and if he did not do it, then someone else would have.

Pastor Craig was a gifted pianist and worked in Nashville before he became a pastor. Many of his family members were still active in the music business that played in the church.

There were a lot of Nashville connections to the church and I was excited when Phil Driscoll, a well-known trumpet player came each year and performed in concert. The church fueled my passion for music and the trumpet. I was given musical solos and played *Amazing Grace, Because He Lives,* and many other Bill Gaither songs on Sunday mornings.

Mom was a stern taskmaster, yet she had a contagious laugh. She laughed until tears flowed. She was a tough, strong woman, who probably weighed over 230 pounds. When she told you to do something as a child you had to do it. It wasn't uncommon for her to grab you by the hand to demonstrate what she wanted you to do. I'm glad she never had to do that to me as I was always eager to help and take on more responsibilities.

In the early 1960s, my mom lived next door to her sister on Custer Avenue in Youngstown, Ohio. She moved to Youngstown in her 20's from Franklinton, Louisiana. She married Clyde Magee and worked at Gilead House Community Center and St. John's Episcopal Church as their child care director for many years. There was never a moment in my mother's life when she wasn't caring for someone.

When my mother's health was failing, there was a sadness that I could not shake. She was such a source of encouragement to me through all of the pains in my life. Her love was overreaching and in her presence, you knew she was praying for you and definitely had your best interest at heart. She had so much compassion for so many kids. Whenever one of us came to her, she knew exactly what each one of us needed to get through the day.

My brother Lee and I decided that it was best to move her and her beloved pure breed toy poodle, Coco, to Greenfield, Massachusetts to be closer to him, and only a few hours from me. I tried to do everything to help her feel comfortable at a nursing facility near Lee. Whenever I had time off, I was there. I spent weekends by her side. Her passing in 2015 left such a void in my life that I never knew existed. There is still a gaping hole that has not been filled.

I'm a person that can always keep my emotions intact. However, during the funeral, after all the local celebrities like the former Mayor of Youngstown, George McKelvey, whom she served as his nanny, and others shared their love for her, I could not hold back the tears. There were many of her foster children in attendance. I was grateful and surprised to see families whom she served as a nanny, pay tribute and share memories. All of the vivid stories and demonstration of love for my mother made it impossible for me to keep a dry eye. This woman from the backwoods of Louisiana, who only attained a second-grade education, made a lasting impression on the world she lived in. Her impact is still felt today.

I don't think mom minded my tears one bit. She was tough to the end and a true Believer. I could almost hear her say, "Wayne, what you crying for? I don't need no tears. I've spent my whole life preparing for this moment,

> *May the work I've done speak for me,*
> *May the life I've lived speak for me,*
> *May the service I give speak for me,*
> *When I come before my Lord,*
> *I want to hear well done*
> *May the work I've done speak for me."*
> **– The Consolers**

My Brother's Keeper
Leander E. Magee
(1959 - 2017)

My brother Lee was several years older than me, and I looked up to him as a father-figure. He was my mother's only biological child. Lee was a genius. He went to private school all his life from kindergarten through college. He attended the famous private boarding school in Hudson, Ohio, Western Reserve Academy. When he went there, he was a year younger than the majority of students and graduated at 16-years-old. Lee then went on to Oberlin College in Ohio.

After graduating from college, he was hired at the age of 20 to teach at the prestigious Deerfield Academy boarding school in Massachusetts. He stayed with Deerfield Academy for over 30 years and taught math and German. He was also the baseball coach and JV basketball coach. Lee was a quiet, giant guy, yet we would speak for hours together in his later years just talking about his life and things he wished he had done.

After burying my mother in the late summer of 2015, a year later, Lee's health took a turn for the worse. He was on dialysis and surgeons removed his fingers, toes, and leg. Despite being two hours away, I was there for him as often as I could. My brother died in January 2017. I was out at sea and could not get back for a week. It was a devastating loss for me and a huge responsibility as I was named the trustee of his estate. There was a lot of wisdom that Lee laid on me in his last year of life after our mother's death, that I often share with others.

There were seven Magee men. After my brother Lee's death, I now wear the title of, "The Last Magee Man." I am proud to represent the hard work, valor, and strength, as I walk in the footprints of those great men.

Defining Moments

*"Have you ever felt trapped in circumstances,
then discovered that the only trap was your
own lack of vision, lack of courage, or failure
to see that you had better options?"*
- **Nick Vujicic**, *Life Without Limits*

In life, you often hear of people's defining moments. Oprah calls it your "Ah Ha Moment." It's in those moments that serve as a tipping point, a definitive mark of resolve and self- assurance. For me, that special moment defined to me that my limits are only the shortcomings of others ill-informed justification, to impose a restriction on what is truly possible in my life. Don't let others dictate your life trajectory.

In my early high school years, I recall being in a school-wide assembly in the newly built gymnasium. The gym was packed as it really appeared that the entire student body was present. We all filled into the maroon and gold hard plastic stands like we often did for the football and basketball team pep rallies. Although, this time the setup was different. I noticed a fairly large protective mat on the gym floor off center nearing stage right. I didn't see the speaker for this assembly until he was announced by Mr. Young, the school's principal. To my surprise, he was a young man, not too much older than us high schoolers. He stood tall and proud, yet he had no hands or feet. His arms stopped around his elbow and he had no legs below his middle thigh. I don't recall his entire life story that he spoke of that day, but his presence left a good feeling inside me, that still lingers today. I was face-to-face with someone who most people would view as having a disability or at the very least a disadvantage in life. But this young man with no limbs demonstrated how wrong we were that day.

He presented a simple message of embracing and accepting yourself and those that may not look like you. He encouraged the attentively focused crowd to work diligently no matter what obstacles or limits that were placed before us at birth or otherwise. What really left the student body in shock is what happened during the concluding moments of his talk. He spoke of how he loved to wrestle and how many adults limited him, and exclaimed: "wrestling is something you can't do without arms or legs." Well, he told us how he worked hard and had mentors and other people around him like the wrestling coach at his high school. He also went to his friends that supported him and helped him learn key wrestling moves and the skills it takes to be victorious. Everyone was in disbelief that he could wrestle. This was long before social media and YouTube!

Neither I nor any of the students could comprehend his actions as a reality. He said that he heard of our highly ranked wrestler, Josh at our school. I believe Josh was in the 110 weight class. Now, everyone realized that the large protective mat was going to be part of a dramatic demonstration. He called Josh down to wrestle him and gave Josh the directive to try and pin him to the mat as quick as he could. Well, the match was over before it started. He aggressively man-handled and pinned Josh in what seemed to be under two minutes. The gymnasium erupted in cheers. It was determination, belief, hard work, tenacity, and skill, all playing out right before our eyes. We all saw what we thought was impossible. It was the most life-changing event that I had ever attended.

Shortly thereafter, I heard a similar testimony by Nick Vujicic, an Australian motivational speaker born with tetra-amelia syndrome, a rare disorder characterized by the absence of arms and legs. I really connected with Nick's story of faith, family and learning to first accept himself, which led to the truth of living his life without limits. Nick is a professional speaker, author, husband, and father. Originally, all of these roles were limits put on him by others that such a diverse and successful life was impossible. I often use Nick's journey, and what he has overcome and achieved as a source of encouragement in my life. I envision myself as a husband and father in the near future. If we want to be tenacious, it must first take form through defining moments in our lives. We must then use those moments as a point of no retreat to the limits that others or society places upon us.

CHAPTER 5

Tough It Out
Be Tenacious

"If you are an effective manager of yourself, your discipline comes from within; it is a function of your independent will. You are a disciple, a follower, of your own deep values and their source...."
– Stephen Covey

A s much as I had been teased growing up, I used to imagine that I was a tenth-degree black belt in Karate like Chuck Norris. On a clear sunny day, I walked along the streets of Youngstown and took care of all the bullies with my expert precision skills and made them apologize to those they hurt. Then, I'd finish out my day at the local Pizza Hut with a personal pan pizza and a cup of lemonade with no ice. It was a fleeting fantasy that I crossed in my mind every now and then, but, *Who was I kidding?* I often thought. I'm not a physical fighter, but I am strong and good with my hands. I'm definitely a fighter emotionally and mentally. If any of my bullies would have cornered me for a fight, although I may not have won, they would definitely know that they had been in a fight. I never sought to knock someone out physically, but I don't think those bullies realized that I am a lot tougher than I look!

I know that it used to frustrate Mr. Allen, an Army veteran when I told him I was being bullied at school. He really wanted to beat up the bullies for me or give me the skills to beat them myself. Instead, the more we talked, the more things made sense as he showed me how to solve my own problems. He taught me self-discipline, which made me tougher on the *inside*.

What does it mean to be tenacious? It means keeping a firm hold, persistence, or not relinquishing a position. When I think about it, I have been tenacious and disciplined in everything I've put my mind to. Since I was different from the others around me; meaning I looked physically different, I wore khaki pants and golf or button-down dress shirts, I was an introvert, and I wasn't at all athletic. I clearly stood out.

Yet what I had that most kids at school didn't have, was my strong faith which led me to believe in myself even when no one else did. Every negative word that was said about me behind my back or to my face, I turned it into a positive moment to propel me forward. I worked harder on my academics. I practiced the trumpet every day. I studied music. I joined every band in my area. I made every moment of my life count, and you should also.

Being Tenacious is the type of characteristic that can help

you become better at self-leadership and being successful. Any adult who remembers me growing up will always say how serious I was about my life. I carried a briefcase in high school and dressed like an adult. I was totally annoyed with how the kids at school fooled around so much and did not take life seriously. I considered myself an old soul and was never one to complain or ever say the words "I can't." Being Tenacious means doing your best to remove "I can't" from your vocabulary as it relates to learning something new or going to the next level.

As a lifelong learner, I enjoy reading works of great philosophers. In *The Story of Philosophy: The Lives and Opinions of the World's Greatest Philosophers*, author Will Durant writes in his discussion on Aristotle, "You are what you repeatedly do. Therefore excellence should be a habit, not an act." I believe Durant's analysis of Aristotle's life and teachings demonstrated that one of the wisest men of all time knew even way back then that living TOUGH, gaining success and seeking opportunity at its essence, comes through excellence in the ordinary - what you do and how you do it daily is the key. Therefore, success equals preparation, patience, wrapped in excellence, to position yourself for your opportunity.

A prime example of this in history is the biblical story of Joseph. Joseph was the second youngest of his father Jacob's twelve children. Out of jealousy, his older brothers sold him off into slavery. As you read Joseph's life story, you will find the constant theme of tenacity. No matter the situation, no matter the false accusations, turmoil or setbacks in his life, Joseph did not retreat with a "woe is me" attitude. His reverent and belief in his dream from God, despite being in prison, kept his hopes for a turnaround high. Joseph's attitude and his preparation, along with his excellence in dealing with others despite his challenging circumstances, allowed him to grab an opportunity when it was bestowed on him.

His diligence in the "ordinary" enabled him to shine. After being sold into slavery, Joseph climbed the ladder of opportunity from a simple Hebrew slave managing other slaves in prison, to the supervisor of an Egyptian government official's house, and then second in command over all of Egypt. When seeking an opportunity, your attitude will affect your altitude. In reading Joseph's journey you will see that it didn't happen overnight! The right opportunity can test your patience. Although he was wronged and forgotten, his attitude and exemplary patience prepared him to lead. His ability not only to wait but, to wait without bitterness, led to even greater success. Joseph is a great example of what will happen when you bloom in the area you are currently in. It is the secret to allowing opportunities to transplant and transport you to where your purpose and dreams lie.

A more recent example of an individual being tenacious is seen in the bravery and sheer boldness of a young Pakistanis girl, Malala Yousafzai. Malala shared her story of her country's tradition that when girls are born, there is not much of a celebration. However, her father was a teacher and he was determined to give her every opportunity boys had. She loved school and learning. In 2008, the Taliban took over her village and banned girls from learning. When Malala became a teenager she began speaking out publicly on girls' right to learn. She became a target of the Taliban and one day a soldier boarded her bus and asked for her by name. The soldier shot her point blank on the left side of her head. Malala underwent extensive surgery in England. Not only is she a walking miracle, but she is also an advocate for girl's rights and continues to speak for girls across the globe. Malala is a bestselling author, speaker, activist and business owner at only 22 years old.

Being Tenacious also means that you have to be a person with moral values and diligence to see your goals through completion. I was fortunate to have Mr. Allen early in my life and a few other mentors later on. Find your mentor. Someone who will hold you accountable for your actions. Mr. Allen and my older cousin, Charles Russell, kept me on my toes. They often reminded me of a few basics to being tenacious:

1) Don't look for the easy way out. Anything worth doing or becoming is going to challenge you.

2) Be authentic, open and honest with your accountability partner. Don't try to hide things that are really bothering you. You cannot achieve greater levels without first acknowledging what's distracting you from your goals, followed by accepting your current status.

3) Challenge your accountability partner and others not to be soft on you in areas where you are weak.

4) Never stop asking questions. Strive to be a continuous learner.

5) No matter how large or small the task, put forth your best effort.

6) Humility goes a long way.

In spite of my current role as a leader, I am intentional in everything I do. I strive to be tenacious each day. Nothing means more to me than being accessible to my students, a team member that my colleagues can depend on, and helping others. Whatever your personal and professional goals, being tenacious at each step will bring you closer to completion and bring a strong sense of fulfillment along the way.

CHAPTER 6

Opportunity Knocking
Seek Opportunity

"Opportunities are like sunrises.
If you wait too long you'll miss them."
– William Arthur Ward

I can't stress enough the importance of preparing for your next goal. Even when I wasn't sure of where my career would take me, I stayed active in the one thing that I was passionate about; playing the trumpet. Not only did I play in bands, but I also played on Sundays, sometimes at two different churches. I never lost focus of my goals even while working as a cook at Charley's Philly Steaks. Keep in mind that I had already graduated from Youngstown State University with a degree in Music, yet I was struggling to find a fulfilling career opportunity.

Every free moment I had I was scouring the internet and the newspaper "Want Ads" for jobs that I believed I was qualified for. If there were skills that I did not have, I researched them and worked towards obtaining them. You can do the same thing. If you are going to take on the tenacious mindset, then you must be open to continuous learning to solidify your path which will give you future career options.

1) What types of preparation can you start today to be ready for your next opportunity?

2) Where are you now and where do you want to go? Write out your current status along with your short-term and long-term goals.

3) Dress the part for your career today!

4) Set up a realistic schedule to work on your skillsets and goals. There are plenty of free online courses to help increase your knowledge. A degree may not always be the vehicle to get you where you want to go.

5) Be willing to sacrifice free time with friends and hanging out. You will have to give up, to go up to where your dream lives.

6) Be open to constructive criticism and learn from it.

7) Inquire and network with others for opportunities based on your talents. Oftentimes, it is not what you know, but who you know, that will give you the chance for an opportunity and your preparation to meet.

If you are really unsure of what path to take ,consider volunteering in your community .Even if it's just for a one-day event .The goal is to be actively involved with others in order to expose you to career options ,local businesses and leaders, or needs in your community that you might realize are available for you to help .I made a point to volunteer at my church every chance I got .It made me feel needed and valued while I was still searching for my dream job .I know first-hand that finding new opportunities is hard work and takes patience .Yet if you stay proactive ,and do your best in your current position ,an opportunity beyond your wildest imagination will appear within your reach .It's up to you to be prepared to grab it.

Push-ups Against Fear

*"When fear is knocking at the door, send
faith to answer and no one will be there"*
- Dr. John Hagee

I can't think of anything I've learned of value that was not hatched in discomfort. Whether it was learning to ride a bike, conducting my first concert band in high school, starting a business, or asking that special someone on a date. Fear and discomfort were real. As I was advancing in my career, I was required to make more presentations. For me, my discomfort and fear was public speaking. I dreaded it, but not to the point where most people fear it over death. I knew I had to face it. I tried everything from writing every word I wanted to say down and rehearsing it to even imagining everyone in the audience in their underwear, which is something industry experts advise. Nothing really worked. I stumbled through speeches at worst or sound like an automated robot at best.

Things changed when a TEDx video crossed my path called, "Speaking Up Without Freaking Out," by author Matt Abrahams. I listened intently to the video and found out later that it was only a few tips from his book with the same title.

Without hesitation, I ordered Matt Abrahams' book from Amazon. It was in my hands in a few days. I started reading it and devised a plan after understanding physically and physiologically what caused my discomfort with speaking. The nervousness, the overthinking, the feeling of being unprepared, all became easier to work on after reading the book. The first tip I recall and one that I adopted without question was called "Push-ups!" Abrams advised that most people who speak for a living had pre-speaking rituals, all of which normally included physical activity. Some ran in place, did push-ups, or recited tongue twisters. These activities were tricks of the mind to help you remain calm and focused. The insights from this book changed my life.

He also talked about breath control. He suggested taking a big breath when you feel anxious during speaking. What really helped me was the importance of realizing your body language when you speak publicly. He mentioned that most nervous speakers make their bodies small by having their shoulders and elbows tucked in, and their head is slightly lowered. This type of body language communicates fear and is heard louder than anything else you may say verbally. Instead, open arm gesturing with open legs and shoulders is a more confident stance and your body now matches your words and helps lessen the anxiousness.

What was interesting about this book is that a lot of what was being said and the science behind it is what I was taught and used as a musician. I just never applied it to public speaking. Never discount the value of reading. The more knowledge you gain will help you push-up against discomfort towards ultimate success.

Uber-ing for Growth

Now, when you think about Uber, the ride-sharing company, you may visualize the phone app you use for rides hailing from the airport or around town. You may also think of Uber as a means to earn extra cash by helping people in your area get to where they need to go. But, during the summers, I saw Uber as a vehicle for a self-paced education; a master class in the art of conversation, presentation and connecting with an audience.

Before Uber, I was a person who did not excel at holding a conversation with a stranger beyond "Good morning" or a common transactional exchange as necessary. Joining Uber was a do-or-die type situation. I was going to push myself beyond the fear of discomfort and engage with those in my car as I drove them to their destination. I forced myself to ask them great questions about their jobs, school, passions, religion, and family. I wanted to engage in good conversation that would be meaningful to both parties. I became tactful in the art of taking the conversation beyond the trivial if the rider allowed. I wanted passengers to leave my car with a smile on their face, and an encouraging word in their heart. Sometimes I wanted to leave them with thoughts to ponder when they were alone.

I considered driving for Uber an honor and act of community service to those I rode in my modest black sedan. I was not driving for the money. I knew going into it, after doing the math, that I would break even at best. I made it my goal to do a few rides a week during the summer months, which became my summer college classroom. I recall riding around young executives to and from the airport, couples and families on vacations on old Cape Cod, and even those down on their luck. This by no means was an easy feat. I had to work on my conversation, pushing myself beyond the fear of possibly being rejected with each rider.

I have so many great and memorable Uber stories. I recall driving a mother of two to the grocery store. She was staying in the local weekly motel, as she was looking for permanent housing in the area. I was able to encourage her and give her resources to agencies to assist her with housing. She was so grateful for the information and the fact that I had a clean car.

One evening, I picked up a couple from Boulder, Colorado, who were visiting friends on the Cape. The couple did not want to burden their friends and ask them to drive to the airport which was about an hour away. Their friend dropped them off at the local shopping mall where they wanted to do some quick shopping before heading to the airport. The couple had horrible luck that day. They called two or three Ubers all of which arrived, but once they found out where they were headed, they canceled. Other drivers told them that they didn't have time to go that far out of town. Many Uber drivers don't want to take trips an hour away. I didn't mind. I picked them up and they were so happy! Now we were on a race against the clock to get to the airport because of the previous Uber cancellations. They had only one hour before their plane would be boarding. During our drive, we had the best conversation about life. The wife was a real estate agent and the husband was a corporate executive. I asked them what was their secret to making a marriage work. Without hesitation, they opened up and shared that making time for one another daily was key. The wife was also a great resource for me as I was walking through selling my brother's home after his death months prior. With all of the highlighted negativity in the world, it's nice to know that there are plenty of kind, hardworking, decent people within our reach.

Later, I once had the honor of driving a diligent college student, Sarah. She was an artist and worked at a local diner and creamery waiting tables. She was wise beyond her years and we connected immediately over our mutual love of art and music. She had a plan to go to art school, but to do it debt free. She was enrolled at the two-year local community college, paying cash as she went. All the while studying her craft and showing and selling her art on the side. I was able to share my story with her of debt-free living and encouraged her to keep doing what she was doing. I know she will reach her dream one day, and when she does, I can proudly say I was Sarah's chauffeur. When she was about to exit my car, she said, "this was the most enjoyable and encouraging Uber ride I have ever taken." She thanked me and smiled. This was so rewarding. Pouring into the generation after me!

Whenever I picked up leaders, I went into full interview mode. I asked them about their leadership style, leadership challenges in the workplace and how they overcame them. I questioned them on workplace culture and how their leadership shaped or influenced staff behaviors. It was a great feeling when people felt comfortable sharing insight into their leadership strategies and employee engagement. Sometimes I was able to move the conversation to a topic of faith, and many believed in a higher power.

I remember talking to Ryan, a young Engineer, that I picked up after he interviewed at a design engineering firm. He was a food engineer for a major brand. However, he wanted to move into the design aspect of engineering. Ryan and I had a half-hour ride. We connected easily as he was a recent college graduate and I worked in higher education. During our conversation on his career aspirations, I felt we had enough rapport to go a little deeper. I asked, "When you were a kid – did you go to church?" He answered "Yes." I then asked, "what does it mean now that you are older?" He stated, "it was everything to me as a Christian." We then talked about the importance of sharing our faith and the reason for our hope in God. He was so encouraged by our conversation that he began asking me questions. "What can I tell one of my co-workers who is skeptical about the authenticity of the Bible?" he inquired. I was able to share with him quick facts about the Bible. Most importantly, I was able to give him a book and a gospel tract on it that I happened to have in my car. The book was written to the skeptic. Ryan told me he was elated we talked that day and even happier to have this new resource for his co-worker, "One Heartbeat Away" by Mark Cahill. Ryan later wrote in the Uber app on my review page about how he was blessed and encouraged after riding with me.

I still drive for Uber from time-to-time. I gained so much from driving people around and hope that the insights and encouragement I offered were helpful. The experience gives me so much joy. I learned first-hand what's on the other side of discomfort - knowledge and human connection.

SECOND MOVEMENT

Slow - Adagio; Middle School - High School

Marching to my own beat...

CHAPTER 7

Bitten by the Trumpet

"Know who you are and dress accordingly."
- Dr. Mike Gervais

Some people spend their entire life trying to find their passion. Mine consumed me during my junior year in high school. I knew with great clarity what I wanted to do for the next *forty* years of my life. Forty was a significant number because I later found out that the maximum number of years you could serve in the armed forces right out of high school is forty. I wanted to spend my life making music in the U.S. Military. My drive and vision became clear immediately after the U.S. Air Force Jazz Band, Airmen of Note from Dayton, Ohio, came and played a concert at Liberty High School. There was only one black trumpet player in the band and his sound was big and brassy. I was awestruck. He made what he did representing the U.S. Air Force around the world both intriguing and inviting. I sensed that he was not operating for his own self-gratification. Instead, it was like he viewed his role as an honor and privilege to represent his country.

As the concert was nearing a close, the band leader asked the students for final song requests. Several students shouted, play the "Sesame Street" theme song. Based upon the crowd's unanimous decision, the band agreed. The band leader provided a disclaimer that they had never practiced it before, but he was willing to give it a try.

At that moment, with the flawless version of the "Sesame Street" theme, as performed by the famous Maynard Ferguson and his orchestra blaring in my head, I set my sights on plans to make it where the sole black trumpet player was in life. I made a decision to do whatever it took to get into the U.S. military band program to serve this country doing what I loved more than anything - playing the trumpet and making great music. My only challenge was to prove to the military that despite my rare genetic disorder, I was strong and able-bodied enough to pass any physical, and intelligent enough to pass any written test they threw at me.

Never one to waste time, while the Air Force Band was still on stage and bowing for their second standing ovation, I went straight to the band room to imitate the life-changing performance I just saw. It was as if I was watching a musical magician. The black trumpet player performed something I had never seen done live. During a ballad, he played two trumpets at once, with each trumpet playing different notes and rhythms at the same time. Besides the minimal light backing of the band behind him, he was almost accompanying himself.

I spent the next few minutes in the band room with my

trumpet and a school-owned old cornet. I tried to play them both simultaneously as I had just witnessed moments before. I had very little luck with getting much of a buzz out of either instrument. I tried a few more times and the sound equated to nothing good. I took a deep breath and convinced myself to try one more time. Just as I blew the cornet, the magician trumpet player, along with a few other Air Force band members walked through the band room because it was connected to the school auditorium. They chuckled when they saw me and pointed to the trumpet player, "See, look what you did!" as they strolled through to their bus out back. That brief encounter became one of the most memorable moments in my life.

From that day on, graduating from high school could not happen soon enough. My entire junior and senior year were centered around going straight into service with the U.S. Military as a musician. An even bigger challenge that I did not foresee was that my mother did not want any part of military service for me. She wanted me to finish college first. She did not believe the military pitch that I could just play the trumpet. She said, "you can't be in the military and just play trumpet for Uncle Sam! They're tricking you and you will have to carry a gun!" To appease her and stop the banter which went on for a few weeks, I caved in, "Ok mom, you win. I'm going to college." I was still determined to go into the military. I just carved out a temporary detour. Even though I later found out that she was right. After basic training, everyone has to be assigned to some form of duty requiring using a gun, other weapons and being adequately prepared for war. At 17 years old you really think you know more than your parents. I was extremely naive and blinded by the magnitude and prestige of playing trumpet for the U.S. military.

Either way, I still had to focus on my music, so I was involved in three different bands simultaneously. I played for my high school band, and two other community bands: The Warren Junior Military Band and the Stambaugh Youth Concert Band. I also played trumpet for many churches in the area. On some Sundays, I played at three different churches, for three different denominations all on the same day.

I also dressed for my role as a band member. I never wore clothes that were less than business casual. I eliminated all jeans and shorts from my closet. This was all influenced by the many music professionals I was surrounded by in all the bands I played. They said, "Don't wait until you get older to be a teacher, a scientist, or whatever you want to be. Do it now! Act the part, learn what someone did to get there and do it!" I constantly tell my students to take steps toward their future today. There will never be a perfect time to start; tomorrow is not promised to anyone!

"You can't have change without process."

I was doing the college thing against my will and I only applied to *one* school down the road from my house. I admit, the college process was challenging, as I had no guidance from counselors at school. I knew music was what I wanted to study and the best and one of the oldest music schools in the country was a mere 3.2 miles away from my home; Youngstown State University (YSU) Dana School of Music. The campus was literally a 5K run from high school. The school's close proximity to home certainly made my mother happy.

I was blessed to have Dr. Christopher Krummel as a trumpet teacher in high school. He gave me trumpet lessons during my junior year, and into my senior year. He was the trumpet professor at YSU. Dr. Krummel began preparing me for the audition to gain acceptance into the music school. I met with him for months, once a week for free lessons during the evenings after school. He guided me through the process of applying to both parts of the school. I did not realize that there was a two-step admission process: I had to apply academically and be admitted into the university first, and then audition for entry into the music program. I was accepted into both programs and received a partial academic scholarship. Looking back, it was all part of my predetermined life's journey. I never gave a second thought that I would not be admitted to YSU, so I did not have a back-up college or alternative plan. My confidence and determination to succeed despite the odds are what keeps me moving forward to the next goal and has made me tougher with each step.

CHAPTER 8

Earning my Keep

"Initiative is doing the right thing without being told."
– Victor Hugo

I can't think of a point in my life where I was in a crisis and needed my mother's help. When it came time to apply to college, I did it on my own and worked with the college administrators. However, a few times, my mother pointed me in the direction of various careers based on her connections. She once was a nanny for a doctor, so she had me visit with the doctor to see if that was a potential career path for me. During the first visit, the doctor told me about the hard work and schooling required to be a doctor and the satisfaction of helping people in times of need. By the second visit, he talked about being able to handle working with blood. I was done. I realized that by that time I had spent my entire life at doctor's visits and nine times out of ten, the intern had no idea what my condition was since cleidocranial dysostosis was something they apparently glossed over in medical school. In fact, many interns never heard of it. So I hated going to the doctor, disliked the sight of blood and I can't even watch scary movies or violence. So being a doctor was crossed off of my list.

My next door neighbor was a starving artist, so I knew that career path was not for me. My mother wanted me to find out answers on my own and not base my future just from her knowledge or connections, as she was in her mid-sixties by this time. I was never worried about whether I would get into college, as my grades were above par, not to mention that my trumpet playing was improving each year as well. I was also armed with key life lesson examples from my mother, older brother Leander, and gleaning what I could from other adults. After high school, I felt like I was prepared to take on the real world.

One good skillset is that I was always a saver. I remember taking a great home economics course back in eighth grade on how to write a check and balance a checkbook. I learned the basics of personal finances and quickly grasped the saver and giver concepts. I also learned the value of budgeting, and how it allowed you the freedom to spend within your means. Once these two concepts resided in me, I always had a stash. Being raised by a single black woman without much money, we were poor and I didn't know it until I was 12 or 13 years old. When things got tight around the house, I helped pay bills. I paid the light bill when we were short. My mom hated taking my lawn or snow shoveling money, but we needed it. I had to step up and help in any way possible. Even in grade school I had an entrepreneurial spirit and sold origami for fifty cents. I was great at making cranes and paper balloons. In college, I got into eBay and bought stuff cheap and sold it overseas in Japan and Europe. This was was my college money for gas and other necessities. I also started buying trumpets and sold them in Europe because they were in high demand. The European market was my niche.

Stop, Look & Listen

I was always the smallest and the youngest one in the house. The real runt of the family, from birth to my teenage years. I attribute my success in life to earning my Ph.D. at home. I learned what *not* to do, based upon watching others in the house. My mother believed in corporal punishment a.k.a "whippings." Most of my siblings got a lot of whippings, but it did not change their behavior. Mom actually made you go out back and get your little brown "switch" from our green and well-wooded acre plot. She whipped me once, but I honestly cannot remember what it was for. It was a one-time slip-up for me because I was known in the house for being a "goody-two-shoes."

I recall a whipping incident of my foster brother who was known for being very reckless with the truth. He took fresh baked cookies from the kitchen without permission. He didn't get a whipping for stealing. Instead, he got a whipping for lying about it. My mother always said, there were two things that she hated more than anything is: "a liar and a thief!" It was from situations like that where I learned the power of truth and keeping your hands off what wasn't yours.

The other kids in the house often said, "You were always the good one. You were the favorite because you were always in the hospital!" I guess in their minds they believed my mother felt sorry for me since I was sick often. But as I gained my strength and tough mindset, my mother trusted me to say and do the right thing. My siblings and the other foster kids in the house called me the "little tattle-tale", which I was *indirectly*. I never went out of my way and told my mother on the others. However, if she asked me if I saw one of them do something, you'd better believe I told the truth! I always thought I was being smart. Not a tattle-tale, but operating in pure survival mode.

Given the breakdown in the house, I was somewhat of a loner and spent more time practicing my trumpet and doing homework. When we went to parties or gatherings as a family, I brought my trumpet with a mute and a nylon rope to practice music and knot tying. Each time we attended outings with social services to amusement parks or water parks, I just grabbed a good seat and people-watched. I hated rides and since I had terrible ear trouble and constant infections, water park fun was always out of the question.

Instead, I relished in sitting around adults learning about marriage from listening to their spouse's horror stories. I learned to watch people and listened to how they spoke to others, which gave me a sense of their true self being revealed. My mother often shared with the new foster families her love for kids and the importance of rules and discipline.

> *"Decide what you want, decide what you are willing to exchange for it. Establish your priorities and go to work."*
> **- H. L. Hunt**

I think most people would view growing up as a poor kid raised by a single mother struggling to make ends meet put me at a disadvantage but I never saw it that way. I was blessed, fortunate at best. I literally had a front-row seat to wealth and power. The fact of the matter is that my mother moved to the suburbs in the '70s from Youngstown after Youngstown State University (YSU) bought her and her late husband, Clyde Magee's, two houses they owned on "Custer Street." It was part of YSU's expansion of the growing university. The houses they owned are now where the university's football stadium, "The Ice Castle," lies today. Ironically, it's the same field I marched on as a member of the university's marching band. The sale of their homes to YSU allowed my mother to make a down payment on a home in a great neighborhood in the suburbs of Youngstown, Liberty Township.

My location allowed me to obtain a good education and form a self-ethic based upon the actions of those in power and wealth literally outside my doorstep. At the age of 12, there were a few state level and local public leaders as my neighbors.

I could throw a stone to a U.S. Senator's home and the State Attorney General's home with one cast from my front door.

What I remembered most about my early teens was the public falls of so many individuals suffered at their own hands. These were great people and good leaders. I went to school with their children. They had the respect of nearly the entire state and local community. Watching their demise from abuse of alcohol and drugs more than changed me from that point on. I saw how men in leadership, with families, lose everything over their actions. Alcohol appeared to be the commonality of their downfall. At the age of 12, I decided I would *never* do drugs or drink a sip of alcohol for the entirety of my life. Shortly after making that decision I recalled reading the Bible and the words of King Solomon, the wisest and wealthiest man who ever lived on this Earth, wrote that wine is a mocker (Proverbs 20:1) and alcohol is not for those in leadership to desire (Proverbs 31:4). Those words and the lives I saw destroyed, solidified my self-worth and has guided me to this day. The early decisions you make about your life's direction can help you or hurt you. It's up to you to decide which path to follow.

Awakening the Gift

In middle school, I really woke up to the world around me when it came to the power of knowledge. It was when music entered my life in the 6th grade, my world changed for the better, and so did my academic standing. I went from a "D" and

"C" student even with the learning disability teachers help to an "A" and "B" student. It was fueled by a challenge. My learning disability teachers thought that I could not balance music/band class and academics. So, I told them to let me give it a try and see what I could do. I still recall my first band class. I had taken a couple of beginner one-on-one and group lessons with the band teacher, who was a trumpet player himself, Mr. Vitullo. Then it was time for me to sit in my first real band rehearsal for the 6th-grade band. I sat down in the last chair in the trumpet section. I was barely able to read music fast enough to play. I was definitely behind musically, as everyone else already had a full year of band at the least.

The band played an elementary edition of the music from the Mozart's classic, "Eine Klein Nachtmusik". This was the song that changed everything as I sat through practices trying to learn how to better read the music, and understanding how it encumbers math, numbers, reading, and logic. My love for math increased and I ended up being an "A" / " B" student in middle school.

I loved art classes and later excelled in English and history as well. In high school, I took advanced courses in history and nearly took every math course the school taught, just because I enjoyed it and I had an option of study hall or take more classes. I hated the idea of study hall in school and I had to endure one for a semester. However, given my love for learning math, music, history, and art, I could have graduated from high school early by the first semester of my senior year. I used the last half of my senior year to prep for college. I began working at the middle school in the band room with Mr. Summers. I tried to get as much experience as I could in this music world before I entered college.

It was these years that I struggled to learn how to learn. I realized that I was not a slow learner, but I learned material differently than my peers, even those in the learning disability classes. I was a visual, tactile learner. I needed to see it logically and to almost touch it and experience it to help me learn. For example, spelling was very difficult for me until I first understood what the word meant and heard how it would be used in a sentence. Then I needed to physically write the word over and over on paper. I would often write the word horizontally and then vertically. It took a lot of time for me, yet once the word was locked in, it was there to stay.

Math was the same way. At that time, I just saw math as patterns and numbers. I discovered mathematical laws and theories that helped me understand complex problems. My 7th-grade math teacher, Mr. Perry, was the first teacher that demonstrated his passion for what he taught. He knew math was powerful and he wanted everyone in his class to know how it worked. He taught his class without any of us ever using a calculator. He taught us to manipulate the numbers whether decimals or fractions to get to our conclusion, all by just using our heads.

For example, he would say to the class, "tell me what's 26% of 8." He expected us to tell him the answer within seconds. He really made math fun, and applicable to the real world. It is because of him, that I literally use mathematical analysis to help come to an understanding of many things in life. I didn't just learn math, I ended up having a lifelong love affair with math. Once I took higher math classes in other grades, such as Algebra, Trigonometry, and Calculus, I did extra homework problems just for fun! In the summer, I wrote out equations and solved for "X" just because. I played with numbers throughout the school year. As soon as I got home from school, I would turn on *Bonanza* and start working on math problems. For me, math was like having dessert *before* dinner.

Safety in Numbers

Again, being in the Boy Scouts were some of the best years of my life. I owe a lot of my success to the men, the fathers, in the program who shared their wisdom with all the boys in the troops. They told us what manhood was, but more importantly, they lived it out in front of us. I took mental notes on how these men treated their wives and kids, especially when they thought no one was watching. There was Mr. Smith, a father with a son and daughter. He devoted his time to us on Wednesdays and treated his wife and daughter to dinner on Saturday; when there wasn't a campout, of course. Then there was Mr. Neuman, the Scoutmaster, a great man, father and husband in my eyes. He always had nothing but kind words when he spoke of his wife. You could see and feel the love he had for his son, Craig, who I went to school with and was in the same Scout troop together. Craig was also a very gifted trumpeter, student and leader. We played in the Liberty High School Band together. He went on to the Air Force Academy and became an aviator, and still serves as an officer today.

There was always an exhibition of love in the Neuman family. Although they had some wealth, the value of hard work was not absent in their home, and a sense of modesty was evident by the old, yet unusual cars they drove. I was clear on the type of man, father, and husband I wanted to be. I knew if I could be half the man that my Scout Masters were, I would be a blessed man when I grew up.

I honestly don't know where I would be if it weren't for my involvement with the Boy Scouts (11 to 18 years old) and the Band (6-12 grade). These activities were safe spaces for me where I was surrounded by "my group," people of all shapes, sizes, and colors that were all headed in a positive direction in life. In these organizations, I was never bullied. I was never singled out or treated differently by the other students or staff. I believe it is important for young people to find their safe place amongst their peers. That place where you are truly equal in contributing to the group or team.

Chapter 9

Shoulders to Lean On

> *"Wherever there is a human being*
> *there is an opportunity for kindness."*
> **– Seneca**

Compared to my peers, I started music late in 6th grade. No lessons. I was playing by ear. Nor did I know how to read music. People are still shocked that I can play trumpet without front teeth. I only wear partial dentures when I am not playing, which I got fitted for during my sophomore year in high school. However, no matter how hard I tried, I couldn't play one note with them in my mouth. It was like trying to run in quicksand. So I carried on playing the trumpet as I first learned - without front teeth. I continued to have teachers invest in me that really pushed me to become better. Within a year, I blossomed in my playing abilities and got stronger reading music.

In life, you may have many people that not only make a good impression on you but make a lasting impact. For me, I was blessed to have a few men in my life that took the time to instill and share their wisdom, and life experiences with me, both good and bad. I can honestly say these men are responsible, coupled with the grace and providence of God, for any level of achievement I have ever obtained. One of these men was my high school band director, Mr. Summers.

When I met Mr. Summers, it was in the August heat of an Ohio summer in 1999. It was my freshman year of high school and his first year teaching in the Liberty Local Schools - a five mile by five mile square, suburban township adjacent to the city of Youngstown, Ohio. I was excited to be part of the high school band and really thought I looked good in my maroon and gold uniform. During that first month of school, I learned a lot about Mr. Summers, mainly his unparalleled work ethic. I never saw a man work harder, with so much passion to help others be their best.

A Summer to Remember

Mr. Summers was responsible for taking our band on our first overnight band camp gig. It was a hot day during band camp in August. The high school marching band was comprised of nearly 100 students. We were bused to the college campus of Edinboro University of Pennsylvania for a five day, four-night camp, to learn the field show for the Friday night football games halftime show that year. Our song selections were a variety of tunes from the '70s, including "Sir Duke," " Build Me Up Buttercup" and "What I Like About You."

We worked hard that summer and one thing that I learned was that it was alright to be passionate about what you do as your life's work. I learned passion was the fuel to ignite cohesion and innovation in those around you. Mr. Summers displayed this to the entire band on more than one occasion. After many repetitious attempts to get the drill and the music together, and believe me, it was just not coming together, he grew frustrated. Standing on a story high scaffolding overlooking the grassy green and white painted football field, Mr. Summers, peeped through his thin steel-framed glasses, and kept providing directives from his megaphone with no improvement. It was actually awful.

At one point, he climbed down and began shouting through the megaphone, attempting to show us by marching *and* tell us what he wanted us to accomplish. After his overtly demonstrative exposition of how it should be done, he gave the command to give it another go. Everyone was shocked. The previous band director had never spoken to us in that manner. We were sure this new guy was going to be nice and not make waves. We attempted the routine again, still with little to no improvement. He was furious. He threw that poor baby blue and white megaphone thirty yards across the field. He was so angry that we were not focused on accomplishing what we set out to do. I don't know if the other band members felt as I did, but he showed me that he really cared for us. I remember how he loudly exclaimed, "I know you guys can do this!" Seeing that sheer passion from him, ignited a fire under the entire band and the next attempt was spectacular. It was almost miraculous!

Going to that band camp in Pennsylvania was the first time I was away from home for music. I was in the Boy Scouts, so I was used to camping out under the stars and being away from home. I was very anxious and excited about the fear of the unknown. While riding on the bus from my high school to the college, my stomach was upset. I must have eaten something spicy the night before. Before I knew it, the bus hit a bump, and I got a sharp pain in my stomach. Without fair warning, diarrhea oozed out in my pants. There was nothing I could do. I just couldn't hold it. I pooped on myself on the first trip with the band.

The bus stank like crazy. The driver asked what happened and everyone thought someone snuck a dog on the bus and it pooped. He let us put all the windows down. As soon as the bus pulled up, to Earl Hall Dormitory, I circumspectly ran to find a bathroom. Fortunately, I found one. However, in between the bus and restroom, when I stood up, I tracked all my poop with me. It was like a breadcrumb trail leading directly to the restroom. I went in and cleaned myself up as best as I could. One of the chaperones saw all the poop in the pathway and then said, "oh some dog tracked all this poop from outside into the residence hall." When I got assigned a room, the first thing I did was jump in the shower, change my clothes and get ready for lunch. I was so afraid of being singled out as the freshman causing all this stink turmoil. I shudder to think of my reputation if I was called out. Luckily, I went undetected. After that near fiasco, I was fine. So far, no one in the school system knows this story, until now. I didn't even tell my mom.

Stepping foot on a college campus as a high school freshman was fascinating and surreal at the same time. The grounds were huge and beautifully manicured. Any place we had to be, there was a long walk, but we fooled around and had a lot of fun along the way. The immense cafeteria choices had my head spinning. I could not choose between pizza, burgers, chicken, tacos, or sandwiches. The variety for this one day of menu options would be at least a week's worth of choices at Liberty High School. I settled for a turkey and cheese sub sandwich, Lay's Barbecue Chips, and a tall lemonade with no ice.

Being in marching band is not for the faint at heart. We practiced at band camp 10 hours a day for five days and four nights. Our schedule in the morning was breakfast, then four hours practice, then lunch. In the afternoon, four more hours practice, then dinner, then two more hours of practice. It was actually a lot easier to focus since we were all together for the same purpose and no one was concerned about going home.

To help us unwind, one night at the camp was talent night. Freshmen were required to participate. This is where my relationship with Mr. Summers came together. Everything in the band is driven by the seniors. I was racking my brain to figure out what I was going to do. Remember, I was very quiet, with no friends, and a new band member. Finally, the light bulb came on and I remembered an old Boy Scout skit that I saw performed at a previous Scout summer camp. I would transform into "The Great Swanee." I ran back to my room and grabbed my burgundy and green checkered bed sheets and dressed up like a fortune teller. I used one of my bed sheets and I wrapped it on my head like a turban and used the other sheet as a cape. I became the wise, all-knowing "Great Swanee." Now, as this character, I did not have a speaking role because "Swanee" does not speak English. I just whispered into the ear of my interpreter, a fellow bandmate named Robert. We quickly rehearsed our roles. Then we randomly selected two band members from the audience to meet, "The Great Swanee" to tell them their future by smelling their shoes.

The first person we called, I unceremoniously smelled his shoe and dramatically whispered into my interpreter's ear that person's future. Then, my interpreter loudly proclaimed to the audience, "The Great Swanee says you will be very rich and famous." We did a similar proclamation for the next person. Finally, the last person we called was Mr. Summers. He came up and took off one shoe like the other two before him. I smelled it. Of course, I dramatically pretended to gag. Then my interpreter leaned over to me as I whispered Mr. Summers' future. My interpreter loudly proclaimed, "You will travel very far!" He then threw Mr. Summers' tennis shoe to what seemed to be a country mile! Everyone cracked up as Mr. Summers went to fetch his shoe. He was a good sport and that opened the door to our mentor-mentee relationship.

Back to Reality

We performed exceptionally well for the Friday night football game. Once school started, Mr. Summers allowed the seniors to lead the band. He was all for student leadership and ownership. Seniors prepared the vision of what they wanted to happen: which songs were going to be performed and other planning details. For my senior year, Mr. Summers allowed me to conduct the band for a concert. In my current role, I also allow students to conduct the band if they so desire. I seek buy-in from my students for whatever the band does. If anything, I pretty much copied Mr. Summer's blueprint for how I treat my current collegian band program. It works well and both my students and I get a lot out of it.

There have been a few times when I've clashed with my administration because they want me to do things that are against the band's desires. For example, since we are a para-military college, the administration prefers military-style marches, and music, which can be boring, especially if you play marches all the time. Everyone can't relate to military marches and John Philip Sousa. I try to mix things up by striking a balance and have my students play pieces that they enjoy with more allowance for artistry. My students are talented musicians that can handle more challenging music and the gratification it affords. I witnessed students in the band not wanting to play, as they were simply hungry for something they could relate to and be challenged. I had to go to bat for my students. On one occasion, I actually used a sports analogy to connect with the administration. I said, "You're asking the band to play tee ball when they are more than capable and have played Major League Baseball. How would you feel if you were asked to play tee ball at 19 or 20 years old?" Luckily, the administration acquiesced.

Mr. Summers' leadership style was truly a compass for me during my high school years and beyond. I am often described as a person of few words. Yet I love conversation and enjoy playing the role of the listener very well. In high school, with Mr. Summers I did a lot of listening. My schedule was two hours of academics in the morning, followed by a concert band period, lunch, then a jazz band period. Then another two hours of academics to close out the day. This was my schedule for the majority of my high school experience. During the lunch period between the two music periods, was Mr. Summers' prep/ lunch time. I helped out in the band room doing whatever was needed from straightening up the chairs to sorting through music. But the most gratifying part of my day was the conversations I had with Mr. Summers. He always provided guidance through sharing his life story with me, because he saw me as a young kid not sure of what he wanted to be in life.

Mr. Summers shared his *why*. Why music was important to him, as well as his musical journey. He was a trumpet player like myself and I believe that commonality created a natural attraction. He shared so many things that I stored, as I took mental notes that would later help me along my musical journey to where I am today. The first of which was, "don't follow the money, but follow your passion combined with your gifts."

Mr. Summers was a wealth of both life experiences and music knowledge. We talked about tons of things. There were also many times when I felt he tried to talk me out of pursuing music. I knew it was because he cared for me and did not want me to experience the cruel rejection of the music business. However, I was always so focused and determined to succeed at whatever I put my mind to, that no one was going to talk me out of my goal. I never took Mr. Summers' "No" for an answer. I was going to find a way to play music no matter what.

One time, during a trumpet lesson he was dissuading me from entering in the Ohio District IV High School Solo and Ensemble Competition. It was the Joseph Haydn "Trumpet Concerto." I was attempting to prepare for a rating. It is difficult, but one of the most popular pieces for trumpet players. I was working on the first movement and having trouble. A lot of colleges and professional orchestral trumpeters have played this piece for auditions. Mr. Summers tried to talk me out of going for a rating. I believed I could get a superior rating of five. Instead, I got a three, which is average. Mr. Summers wanted me to go for comments only, and no rating, but I was determined to get a high rating. I was upset with the three, but not discouraged and I just kept practicing.

Sometimes, the more I expressed my desire to be a musician, the more I felt Mr. Summers was trying to talk me into pursuing a career in math or science. Like I mentioned, as a musician himself, he knew how rigorous and competitive it would be and he didn't want me to get hurt or discouraged. But I was a stickler for learning to play the high note. I wanted a solo high note performance. He's still in disbelief that I can play the trumpet in the first place since the physical act of playing trumpet is to rest the trumpet mouthpiece behind your upper teeth. It's like saying "t" or "v". Without front teeth, it is difficult, to say the least. He often comments on how well I can articulate on a trumpet without any front chompers.

Forgiveness

I was most hurt by the bullying from other black and brown people. The sting was deeper being singled out in the black community, mostly by children and even some adults. Sadly, my biological family members didn't embrace me for being different. They said things like, "You talk white!" They said I had a white nose, and dressed white. Most black people just didn't get me because I was respectful and kind to everyone. I strongly believe that respect and kindness have no color.

The other black kids picked on me for focusing on academics and excelling in school. Aside from the name calling of "butthead," "heart head," or "brainiac," to which I actually didn't mind being called a "brainiac." I did my best to take it all in stride. I didn't focus much on who said what about me because I knew it was just a waste of time. The jocks always had something mean to say, especially when I was wearing my white astronaut-like helmet.

Bullying at school was one thing, but outside of school, it was more hurtful to hear the remarks about not being black enough from my biological family. They even tried to make me more black by buying me the FUBU brand, "black clothes." I tried the clothes on. They were uncomfortable and loose-fitting. I like my clothing to fit my body like it was cut specifically for me. The FUBU outfit was like asking me to wear a costume. I thanked them for the clothing and quickly changed into khakis and a golf shirt as soon as I got back home.

I was laughed at for listening to what they called "white" music like Wayne Newton, Glenn Miller, Pat Boone, and Chicago. I enjoyed classical music too like Bach and Beethoven, which I tuned in to on my local NPR radio station, WYSU. I listened to Lawrence Welk, and country music by Charlie Pride and Hank Williams Jr. My choice of television also opened me up to an onslaught of ill-humored jokes by my family because I loved classic TV shows like *Bonanza, Leave It to Beaver, Happy Days, The Andy Griffith Show* and *Walker Texas Ranger.*

By the time I got to high school, I still had poor self-esteem when I was around my peers. My self-imposed social isolation was due to constant bullying. I can definitely say, it was only my faith and the grace of God that got me through high school. I loved the classroom time in high school but dreaded the social interactions with my peers. It was a rough time. I only felt included with my peers in the band and Scouting. The other high schoolers treated me one of two ways: (i) As a superior like I was a teacher or an adult for whom they had respect (ii) As less than, like I could not comprehend or relate to them.

I'm sure part of my treatment in high school was due to my commitment to being tenacious and tuned in on excelling in music and other academics. I knew God had a purpose for me and I knew He was with me each day. During the hard days when the outcast treatment was unbearable, I complained to my mother about how no one understood me. That no one wanted to treat me like they treated others in the school. No one joked friendly with me as they did with the others. No one invited me to come over to their houses after school. I felt rejected, just for being me, for being who God created me to be. In hindsight, I realize that the wall I created as a young person by not wanting to be a child and rushing into adulthood may have contributed to the other kids treating me like a teacher or a person of authority. By that time, I had spent years trying to be a grown up and now I was upset that kids treated me as such.

Nevertheless, I found solace in my faith. God reveals Himself to everyone in different ways. He spoke to me clearly through His Words in the Bible. The Bible was the only book that I wanted to read and saw value. It was like it read me. It is living truth and I felt that truth at a young age. God would often comfort me when I felt most alone during my schooling years. He brought the words of gospel hymns to my remembrance. Songs like "It is Well," "How Great Thou Art," " Because He Lives," "He Touched Me," "Blessed Assurance," and "Through It All." God still talks to me musically today. Through the *tough blows*, He always points me to His Word and often a song illustrates His presence with me no matter what I am going through.

High school graduation finally came and my mother gave me a party. I met my biological father for the first time. He actually did not live far from me. He gave me a pocket watch with my name and graduation date on it. We only talked for a few minutes because I really didn't have much to say. I was told early on by my relatives that he said, "He did not want a retarded kid." I always remembered those words. When he saw that I was college bound, he now wanted to be part of my life. He called a few times and brought my half-sister over to play. In my mind, this was his way of apologizing, although he never actually said the words. However, his motives for waiting so long and now trying to invest in me after my stock had increased, was for naught. My mind had already closed to starting anew. My focus was on college and I wanted to show him respect as an elder and let him talk. I have no ill-will or hard feelings for my father or anyone who tried to make me feel less than as I was growing up. Yes, I was hurt too many times to count, but I have truly forgiven each and every person who did not see me as a complete gift that God created.

CHAPTER 10

United We Stand;
Embrace Unity

*"Nothing of significance was ever achieved
without people working together."*
– John C. Maxwell

There is nothing like the feeling of being an active member of a positive group. The Boy Scouts and my participation in several bands over the years gave me a breath of life like nothing else. Finding your group is an important step in the discovery process, however embracing unity should be your first step. You want to be where people are united to a goal that is aligned with yours. You want to run in a herd, not against it, which in and of itself speaks to insanity. It would be like you want to be a plumber, yet only hang around carpenters all day. You need to be part of a group that sees the big picture of working together as a cohesive unit. Unity speaks of a shared vision and where there is no unity of a shared vision, there will only be confusion and little if any progress.

To this point, the great leadership expert John Maxwell said it best when he stated, "teamwork makes the dream work." So much more can be achieved in an environment that encourages friendship and support. The fact that each one of us has several gifts and talents, strengths and weaknesses, that when we are united for a common outcome, the likelihood of success in creating "the next great thing," is imminent, as opposed to going at it alone. It's a liberating feeling knowing that our dreams and goals can be accomplished working alongside others.

I deem it a blessing to be in a room where there is the diversity of thought, creativity, and problem-solving techniques being freely utilized. Everyone has the chance to contribute and be of value. As I mentioned earlier, being around like-minded individuals in various bands and the Scouts, gave me new life and a sense of purpose, which ultimately gave me the encouragement to work harder at my craft. It also taught me communication and social skills, as well as how to be a better listener.

In high school, I was fortunate to have the band as one of my core groups. The students of the band were among the top students in the school academically. I felt at home and welcomed when I engaged with most of them in and out of rehearsal sessions. However, amongst my favorite people in the band were two fellow trumpet players whose company I enjoyed because they would stretch me intellectually with every conversation. Ben was Jewish and Ebenge, the son of an African immigrant, were always involved in a civil, yet, spirited debate with one another on politics, history and current world events. They seemly were always on opposite sides of every issue they discussed.

I remember after some time getting to know them and being challenged by them, I exclaimed one day, "you guys have truly mastered the art of debate!" Thus, I called them the "Master Debaters." These two guys sparked such a curiosity in me of the world outside of the four walls of the school building. Their friendship started me on a path to not only have an opinion or conviction on the world around me but, to be prepared to defend it.

I realized that if you desire to change opinions, stereotypes, or even legislation, embracing unity with groups that are different from you and with different viewpoints can result in successful outcomes. History has provided us with great transformational leaders who sought to unite people that were racially discriminated against in furtherance of political goals. Whether we look to Dr. Martin Luther King Jr.'s efforts during the Civil Rights Movement or Nelson Mandela's 27-year incarceration to end apartheid, these two great leaders were always willing to come to the table with those who thought differently than them. They were charismatic, empathetic, knowledgeable, and had the fortitude to fight for the equality of others, at the risk of their own lives.

Early on, I failed to realize that uniting with others could also be a huge learning experience. You get to see first-hand the mistakes of someone in a similar position to where you desire to go. I believe we learn more lessons in failure than in success. Failure should make us want to work harder and stay committed to our goals. It keeps you humble and hungry for more. At the end of the day, I think failure makes you a better mentor or advisor to others because you have already experienced an important challenge. It's one of the reasons that I believe my life story, my successes, and failures, can help others move forward. It really doesn't matter where you are in your journey, whether you in are high school, college, or advancing in your career. There is always an opportunity to start anew and learn from those around you. Especially those coming from different backgrounds. In your efforts to reach another level, if you Seek Unity and Embrace others, the benefits of that connection will more likely than not, flourish to new levels and exceed your expectations.

THIRD MOVEMENT

Minuet/Scherzo (Humor) College

Self-Leadership ...

CHAPTER 11

Mad Dog

"A dream doesn't become reality through magic;
It takes sweat, determination, and hard work."

– Colin Powell

When I arrived on the campus of Youngstown State University (YSU), I was a very focused, yet socially awkward student. I was the most comfortable when I could hide behind the trumpet and let it speak on my behalf. My nickname in college was "Mad Dog." I got the name first from a fellow trumpeter who was in the same class as me. His name was Dennis Hawkins. Now, Dr. Hawkins is a director of bands at Middle Tennessee State University. The initial conversation was very simple but, classic. He said, "Why are you always so intense? You need to relax a bit - "Wayne-o"!" He called me "Wayne-o" too. I told him that I had a goal to make it to the top band at the university. Even though I never made it, I kept trying. After that conversation, he asked If he could call me "Mad Dog." I agreed and the name stuck for the next four years. For those that embraced my differences and accepted me for how I chose to live, they all called me "Mad Dog;" a focused, determined, crazed dog trying to get a bone, not letting anything or anyone stop me.

I always registered for 8 AM classes and was up by 6 AM. I am a stickler for being on time and I was usually dressed and out the door by 6:30. My commute from the suburbs was 3.1 miles and it took me 11 minutes because of traffic lights and the speed limit was only 25 mph. I was at my parking spot near Bliss Hall, the music school before 7 AM. I never really ate breakfast. Instead, I ate more during lunch, usually a *Subway* foot-long sandwich on whole wheat honey oats bread or food I cooked from home, which was normally leftovers from dinner the night before.

After my morning classes, I warmed up for a day of playing the trumpet. Then I headed to concert band rehearsal, followed by marching band practice. With less than an hour break in between, I had two afternoon classes, then Jazz band rehearsal. I played in a lot of music ensembles in college, much more than was required. I enjoyed playing because most of the other students were extremely gifted. They made me practice more just to keep up. After that, if I didn't have a night rehearsal, I went home, cooked dinner and did homework. Sometimes I pulled out the trumpet one last time before bed. This was my routine Monday through Friday while working odd jobs like cutting lawns, yard work, home maintenance or taking on a few music gigs on the weekends.

During football season "Game Day" Saturday's, I was part of the university's marching band at YSU, "The Marching Pride." We played for all the home games. It was an exciting Division I sports environment. I was honored to play a duet with another gifted trumpeter, Mark Gosiewski, during the halftime show that fall of our freshman year. It was exhilarating to have our names announced in a 15,000 seat stadium.

I was gaining more confidence with my trumpet playing abilities. At the same time, Dr. Christopher Krummel was the professor of Trumpet at YSU. I spent at least two hours each week with him during my four years of study at the university. Dr. Krummel has a doctorate (D.M.A.) in trumpet. Not only is he a skilled trumpeter, but he could also tell you the history of the trumpet without missing a beat. Through his life testimony, he taught so many life-lessons many of which I pass down to my students today. The first lesson was to never shy away from something because you have little experience. Yes, it will be challenging on many levels, but the lessons learned trying are invaluable. He illustrated this point by using himself as an example of a young trumpet player when he took a job in an orchestra in Mexico.

First, he was a white male, who did not speak a word of Spanish. Second, he did not know anyone in Mexico. He eventually learned Spanish because he had to eat to survive. He taught me not to fear the unfamiliar but to embrace it. I would later take a similar path a year after graduation from college. I took a job in a different state eleven hours from home, where

I did not know a soul and did not speak the industry jargon. It was what he taught me that made my decision to step out of my comfort zone to an unfamiliar world a welcoming reality.

Another thing Dr. Krummel dropped on me was a statement that I have lived by since the moment he shared it with me. It struck a chord so deep and I could not shake its application far beyond the reach of music. During our weekly lesson, I was playing a difficult music passage. I was trying to completely imitate a famous trumpet player's sound. He told me. "Wayne, it's fine to listen to recordings of many great professional trumpeters, learning how they sound and their approaches to music. But, you don't want to die a mere copy of them. You will always lose resolution with a copy of an original. Why would you want to be known as the trumpeter that is a copy of another? You want to be you, have your own sound!" That was the most freeing thing I had ever heard. His advice set me on a new path to becoming more accepting of myself. I did not care if my sound did not fit in exactly, because I was literally made by God to stick out.

Pushed Beyond Fear

"The shell must break before the bird can fly."
– Alfred Tennyson

Dr. Perkins was my Music Theory teacher at YSU. Being in his class was the first time in my music career that I failed. Being a trumpet player, I never wanted to sing. I had to sight sing and it was very hard for me. I ended up failing the course. He later stepped up as a mentor as he saw that I was not necessarily comfortable with singing. He gave me an incomplete and I made up all the work to get a grade. Dr. Perkins spent an hour each week of his time to train me on sight singing and gave me great techniques on how to do it. He pushed me to get over my fear of singing. In that failure, I was able to succeed the next time around. I have never failed in music after that. I later realized that I could not do it on my own, and thankfully, he graciously offered his help. Although my pride would not let me ask for help, Dr. Perkins cracked my shell and helped me in more ways than one.

The Stairwell

In music school, there are what they call practice rooms. These are padded rooms covered in acoustic sound absorbent titles. For me, entering these rooms was like wearing a straight jacket. It reminded me of when I was younger wearing the little white helmet, that was awkward and restricting. I couldn't practice in a room that small. So, I practiced everywhere else I could find. My favorite spot was the stairwells of "Bliss Hall," the main music school building on campus. The echoes and reverberation of the sound made the most difficult of passages fun to work on. However, from time-to-time, I was halted from my Bliss Hall practice by a professor who let me know that my sound bled into his classroom. When that happened, I either waited until I got home or if it was early fall or late spring, I went to my fallback practice spot on the front stairs of the "Pollock House." It was an old mansion that YSU used for private functions.

There was little foot traffic in and out of the house, so it became my practice house. I sat on the steps perched like a bird practicing my trumpet and sometimes just studying to get out of the air conditioning of the academic buildings. It was during my practices that I noticed people walking by and realized that there was something missing in my life. It was what I now know as "balance" and having "a group" to make the best out of life. Students were engaging each other and working through issues as an accountable group. This is what I was missing, my community - my group. It was then that I began to socialize more, but still with a "Mad Dog" determination to be my best.

Two are better than one because they have a good return
for their labor:
If either of them falls down one can help the other up.
But pity anyone who falls and has no one to help them up.
- Ecc. 4:9-10 (NIV)

CHAPTER 12

Diverse Solutions; Engage Groups

"If you are a rubber band, you need to be stretched to be functional."

I think one of the things I admired the most about Dr. Krummel at YSU was that during our lessons he would sometimes go off on a tangent about politics, or his world view on a certain matter. I often shared my opinions as well. In fact, he welcomed it. He challenged me to present facts for my positions or to search out answers for myself on a matter. I remember him humbly pointing to the diplomas on his wall, urging me to explain or "talk to him" about a musical concept or idea in terms of someone who has a Doctorate in music could ascertain. He always wanted to stretch his students, his rubber bands, to places that he knew was within each of us. Whether on the verbal or technical side of music or playing the trumpet, he believed we had a lot more to offer.

Groups for Growth

"The Proximity Principle: To do what I want to do I have to be around the people who are doing it and the places it is happening."
- Ken Coleman

In my life, any success has come both professionally and personally from engaging those that are doing what I want to do, going where I want to go or have learned what I want to know. I learned early on that enveloping myself in their knowledge would help pave a pathway to my dream. Nothing of any significance is obtained alone. If you ask the most successful people you know about their trajectory, chances are there is a commonality. Like me, they all had an engaged group of individuals to help them get to where they are today from a professional, spiritual and personal development perspective.

I have three groups of people in my life. Each group has its place in a sector of my life to propel me, engage me, and most importantly, keep me accountable. First, I have my professional group. These are people that are on various levels in the working world from retirees to top industry leaders and mid-career individuals. Some of these are both mentor and even mentee relationships; it is reciprocal. I make it a habit to engage these group as a whole or on an individual basis at least twice a year. If you are considering a group like this, make sure it is filled with people you trust to challenge you. This special group consists of people you can share your story with, your *why* and where you want to go because they have been there or are headed in that direction.

My second key group is my spiritual accountability group. This group is also known in most religious circles as a "Connect Group." For me, this is a small group of two to three men that I go to seeking guidance from a Biblical viewpoint. They have permission to call me out if they feel I'm not walking the same way I am talking. You need people to hold you accountable to your religious convictions and integrity.

The last key people in my life is my social group. I actually call this my true friends group. These are friends that you know are there for you regardless of the circumstances. They are supportive of your dreams, goals, and ambitions and should be part of your cheering squad and fan club. Even if you have fallen, these are the people to call when you are in despair, as they are your very close friend group. You can call on these friends anytime, whether you are in the White House (at the top of success) or have been evicted from your house (going through trials). Everyone needs a few key friends in this group.

Finally, I often share with my students that your education and skill set will only take you but so far. It will be more often than not the people that are connected to you in your groups will be the air that causes you to rise to challenges and help you capture your new horizon of opportunity. The truth is, nearly seventy percent of people who land their dream job, will do so because of a relationship that allowed them access to seek the opportunity in the first place. Network to build strong relationships to connect to your future goals.

CHAPTER 13

Gonna Fly Now

---

*"The first step towards getting somewhere is
to decide you're not going to stay where you are."*
– J.P. Morgan

When I was a junior in college, I remember walking down the hall of the music school and I saw a bold black and yellow poster embossed with the U.S. Army logo on the wall about auditions for the U.S. Army Band. I felt a tingling sensation in the bottom of my feet all the way to the top of my head. This was my time! It was my opportunity to audition for the U.S. Army Band for music students interested in serving in the U.S. Army Band and Chorus stationed in Europe. The audition date was scheduled for a couple of months away. I sought out anyone at the university that had been in the military to get insight on what to prepare for in the bands and basic training. Fortunately, Dr. Krummel was an Air Force Band veteran and he was a great resource. Others told me that military basic training involved a lot of running and push-ups and mental head games. I knew I was mentally ready for anything a tough-talking drill sergeant could throw at me.

But, my physical training was definitely lacking. I began doing progressive push-up sets and sit-up training. I started with a set of ten each day and after a week or so, added more sets until I was up to doing about 60 pushups and sit-ups in one sitting multiple times a day. Then came the running. I had run track in middle school for one season, as a sprinter, but distance running was something I knew nothing about. In the beginning, due to my sprinter mindset, I was unable to finish my initial long runs strong. I needed to slow my pace and find something to keep me motivated and focused long enough to run the distance.

I remembered that I had won an iPod my first semester in college during a welcome back give-away. I uploaded the iPod with all of my favorite R&B songs from The Jackson 5, Stevie Wonder, Tower of Power, and I changed things up with The Beach Boys, Frank Sinatra, and Tom Jones. I began doing short runs around the block in my neighborhood, starting on my street, Murray Hill Drive, then I turned into the loop on North Lawn Street, then Fifth Avenue then ended on Academy Drive. After this first round, I then ran the course in reverse. The entire run was a little less than a half of mile. The irony of what makes that run special is the foreshadowing of the final street, which was Academy Drive. This is the same name as the street I currently work on. It is amazing to actually experience God's plan for my life all along.

Once I started running and focused on the pace of the music, I ran for miles with no issues. I always planned my playlist to end my run with the Rocky theme, "Gonna Fly Now." As I neared the end of my run, I sprinted to the finish line of my driveway as fast as I could! I was confident that after those couple of months of training, I could more than max out the U.S. Army Basic Training PT standards. In my mind, there was nothing the Army could throw at me that I couldn't overcome mentally, musically and physically!

"So many times I question the certain circumstances
And things I could not understand.
Many times in trials my weakness blurs my vision
And that's when my frustration gets so out of hand.
It's then I am reminded, I've never been forsaken.
I've never had to stand one test alone..."
– Through the Fire, The Crabb Family

To my surprise, the audition was very simple. The Army came to YSU and used a few classrooms for the audition process. There were two Army bandsmen and a general army recruiter. They wanted me to play a prepared piece and sight read music that they brought with them. I recall it being a quick tempo march and a lyrical sight-reading selection. When it was over, they said they would get back to me and I felt positive because they appeared impressed with my performance. They later contacted me by phone to put me in touch with an

Army recruiter to go through the formal medical process. At that point, they found out I was disqualified. Still not deterred by the Army's "disqualified" reply, I set out on a path to try the other armed forces. I prepared to audition for the Navy and the Marines.

During that time, I had no idea that having CCD and no front teeth would prevent me from joining the military. Once I opened each letter, the moment I saw the word "disqualified" I ripped it to shreds. My "Plan A" to join a U.S. military band and serve in the music field was completely over. I was devastated. Later on, after I recovered from that emotional setback, I researched *why* I was disqualified. I copied this example of my teeth issue, as well as having deformed clavicles due to CCD, that disqualified me in a critical health area of passing a military physical.

DENTAL[1]

The causes for rejection for appointment ,enlistment ,and induction are:

c .**Insufficient natural healthy teeth or lack of a serviceable prosthesis, preventing adequate mastication and incision of a normal diet. This includes complex (multiple fixture) dental implant systems that have associated complications that severely limit assignments and adversely affect**

---

1 https://www.military.com/join-armed-forces/disqualifiers-medical-conditions.html

performance of world-wide duty. Dental implants systems must be successfully osseointegrated and completed.

My main problem was, I never had a Plan B. When you're young, you think everything is going to work out according to *your* plan. I've learned to just keep living. There's a Christian saying, "If you want to make God laugh, tell him your plans!" I knew that God was with me every step of the way on my journey, so after feeling defeated for a few months, I started working on my Plan B. I was still practicing and playing trumpet on a regular basis, I just had no idea what I could do with my passion besides music. *What else was I good at? What else did I really like?* Were my constant thoughts. Then it hit me. *Leadership!* I could carve out a niche by using music to develop the leadership capabilities of students. The number one goal of any leader should be to make more leaders. I wanted to equip, guide and pour into the next generation of leaders after me.

After graduation, I set out on a path to find a job where my passion for leadership and music, along with my skills in administration and helping others, would collide and form a sweet spot in landing my dream job. I considered myself a natural leader, so armed with a degree in Music, I was ready to put my academic credentials to use. I applied for jobs all over the state of Ohio. I sent out hundreds of resumes and received rejection letters each week. *Why can't I get a job? What am I supposed to do?* I kept praying and serving in my church, from the usher board to leadership and hiring committees. I eventually took a job with an upcoming franchise owner at Charley's

Philly Steaks. I knew it wasn't what I wanted for my career, so I kept looking for jobs in between working 30 plus hours a week. I applied to everything I saw in music and all opportunities that had a leadership and administration component to them. Since I did not have a teaching license, my search was limited to private and boarding schools. I sent resumes to any job ad that mentioned music, leadership, management, paramilitary, college and secondary schools.

There were over 50 places where I felt I could use my intersection of music and leadership in various fields. After a year and a half, I had applied to every place in Ohio in line with my goals. Then, I started applying out-of-state. I kept asking myself, *what does God have next for me?* I began to seek God to show me the right place and the right people he would use for his purpose for my life. More than anything, I wanted to be in the right place, with the right people, walking in my life's purpose. I kept hearing the word "patience" during my prayer time. I trusted God's guidance, and after more soul searching and applying out of state, my dream opportunity finally opened up. I wanted to shout out, "Look, mom, I found a sweet spot in a military-style environment, where I could demonstrate my music and leadership skills to help students that did not require me to carry a gun!"

INTERMISSION

Photos

My mom, "Ida the Great."

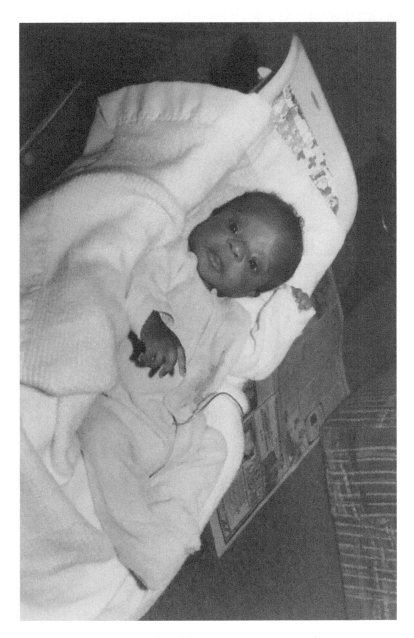

Five months old...gaining my strength

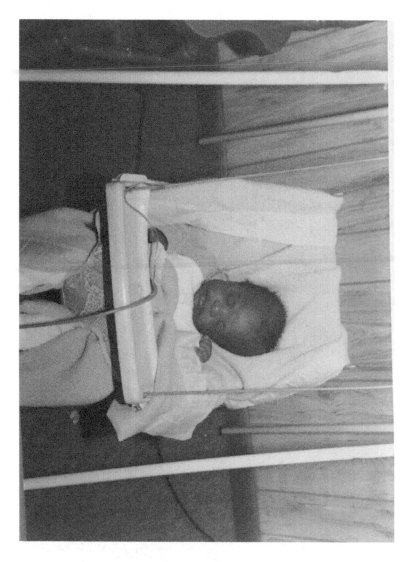

It was a tough day!

At play with my helmet.

Fairhaven Picture Day!

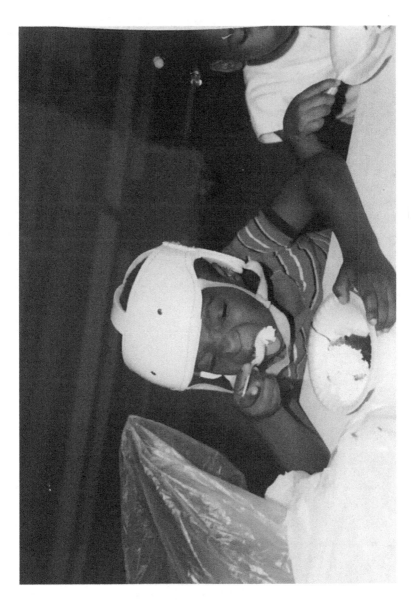

Fairhaven ice cream social.

Boy Scout Camp

A proud Scout!

Liberty H.S. Marching Band Picture Day, 1999

It's official! Adoption day with Judge Swift, 14 years old.

Eagle Scout Press Release Photo, 2002.

Eagle Scout Court of Honor, December 2002.

Warren Junior Military Band, 2001.

Summer 1994 Family photo: Left to Right: Me, Mom,
my brother Lee and my foster brother Marcus.

Thanksgiving 2012: Family Kitchen: Left to Right: Lee, my foster brother Marcus, my sister Courtnei, Me, Mom and my sister Charmaine (center)

New York City Veteran's Parade, 2014

New York City's Veteran's Parade 2014

Lindsay and me at the 2017 Massachusetts Maritime Academy
Ring Dance: Boston Park Plaza Hotel Ballroom

With my love Lindsay. 2017 7th Company
Annual Spring Dance.

Mass Maritime Ring Dance 2017 Boston

Sea Term

Sea term

FOURTH MOVEMENT

Allegro Vivace (Up Tempo); Career Path

Leading the Pack...

Chapter 14

Plan B is for Buzzards Bay

*"For I know the plans I have for you," declares
the Lord, "plans to prosper you and not to
harm you, plans to give you hope and a future."*
– Jeremiah 29:11

I was ready for a change of scenery. Up until that point, I had spent my entire childhood and adult life within a five-mile radius from home. During my job search, I was working at Charley's Philly Steaks which was walking distance from my house. At Charley's, I was a cook and I grilled chicken and steak for the Philly cheesesteak sandwiches. I got along well with the owner as he was new to franchising and decided to give it a try after working at the local General Motors plant. He used money from an early buyout to see if he could make a new living. We were both young; he was in his mid-thirties and I was in my early twenties. It was great to have leadership and business start-up best practice discussions.

I read a job post for the Massachusetts Maritime Academy, located 54 miles South of Boston. I checked the location on Mapquest and it was a 10-hour drive from Youngstown. Everything about the job description seemed perfectly designed for me. I felt an immediate calming in my spirit as I read every word. They wanted someone to teach CPR...check, I am an Eagle Scout. They wanted someone with a music background, band, fiscal management, and student leadership experience...check. I applied via snail mail and it took two months before they called me back. I believe the ad was posted in late November and I stumbled upon it around Christmas. Looking back, the initial intersection of my dream job happened around my birthday, which let me know that God was with me. I was about to be blessed with a special gift that literally entailed the desires of my heart. In late February, I received a call from the Massachusetts Maritime Academy (MMA) to set up an in-person interview.

I was excited about the interview as I knew I was qualified. My mother and I drove to my brother Lee's house, on the beautifully manicured campus of Deerfield Academy, in Deerfield, Massachusetts. This stopover put me three hours away from MMA. I wanted to drive myself, but my mother refused to let me drive her silver and gray Buick Lucerne alone. It was a beautiful car, with grey leather-like seats and a quiet, smooth ride. The road trip was somber at best. Mom was uptight. She felt like she was losing me as if she was sending me off to war. She had mixed emotions because she was happy for me, but definitely did not want me to leave Ohio.

We stayed overnight at Lee's place and woke up early to be at the college by 8:30 AM for my 9:00 AM appointment. Mom sat in the car while I went inside for the interview. By 9:40, I was out the door! At first, I felt a little annoyed. *I just drove 10 hours for a measly 40 minutes!* I thought. But then that calming peacefulness overcame me again. I was in my element. On other interviews, there was always tension and awkwardness. This time it was different. The conversation flowed as though I had been doing the job previously. I interviewed with a four-person panel; Human Resources, Vice President of Student Services, the Dean of Students, and a person who had a similar role that I was going to take on. The position required filling two roles: band director, which included leadership over the honor guard, drill team and serving as one of the residence hall directors. I asked lots of questions and every answer encouraged me that this was the right fit for me. I realized that in essence, this interview exceeded my expectations because I really wanted this job and I was convinced that my sense of passion clearly shone through.

They stated that they would get back to me in two weeks. I felt confident as they informed me that they were the decision-making body with the President of the college having the final word. Within two weeks, I received a call that they selected me. I was elated. When I hung up the phone I ran out in the front yard with the family dog, Coco running after me. I managed to do a few front flips which worked out well, although the backflips flips were definitely a bad decision. As an aside, deep down, I also had aspirations of being a gymnast. I have been known to attract attention on the dance floor at parties as I would groove to the music spiced with a few flips and ending in a full split.

When I received the offer letter in my hand I still couldn't believe it. I really wasn't sure if it was true. Then I shared it with my family. My mother first, and then I called my brother Lee and talked about salary and whether someone could live off the offer amount a year. At that point, I did not know that I could eat all meals on campus which was definitely a plus. I talked again to Lee and my mentor Mr. Allen, about how they handled their money and what I needed to do going forward. Mr. Allen explained retirement benefits and health insurance to me as well.

I still took a few more days to decide if I was really ready to move to Buzzards Bay, Massachusetts. I was still pondering this job offer to work at a maritime college that trained ship captains, and other maritime-related professionals majors. I also had an offer to be a trumpet player on a cruise ship. It felt great to finally have options, and I now had two solid offers in my hand. Of course, I wanted to be a musician and travel, but the cruise ship was only a six-month contract with no stability. I spoke with a few friends from college who went the cruise ship route and they said it was fun, but they would never do it again or for a career. So I ruled it out.

"...Two roads diverged in a wood, and I—
I took the one less traveled by,
And that has made all the difference."
– Robert Frost, The Road Not Taken

After more than ten years at the Massachusetts Maritime Academy, I know I made the right decision. I have been fortunate that the two people on my initial interview panel are still my superiors; the Vice President of Student Services and the Dean of Student Services. I truly believe there is a Godly reason for me to be here. Witnessing my student's accomplishments year-after-year is definitely one of the many pluses. I still have a sense of peace at this stage in my career. When you are walking in your purpose, God will find you a specific place to operate your gift, and then he will send people into your life to confirm it. Do your part and allow him to do the rest.

Chapter 15

Marching Orders

*"The real job of us as leaders is not about being
in charge, but taking care of people in our charge."*
– Simon Sinek

I was one of the youngest full-time hires at the Massachusetts Maritime Academy. At that time, I was only a year older than the graduating class. My office is only two feet from where students live. I am right smack in the middle of a dorm of 200 plus students. One night a week I am on campus for 24 hours. It is something that I love doing. I always wanted to be accessible to the students. I come in by 7 AM and stay until the next day. I often stay until 10 AM because I want to provide the best service I can to the students. I would hate to miss a morning. It is the best time to really connect with the students. I also underscore servant leadership. If that means stacking chairs and moving things around before or after a practice or an event, then that is what has to be done.

Everything I do is with diligence and a sense of urgency. People see me physically in a sprint, often in a brisk jog running around campus every day to get things done. Many students have knighted me "The Black Flash," respectfully, of course, and I accept that label with honor. I could be on the phone with a colleague and they'll ask a question or want to talk about something and I literally drop the phone and run to their office. One of the main reasons why I run all the time is because the doctors said I wouldn't be able to run, and if I did learn to run, it's something I should never do. Every day I continue to prove them wrong.

My typical Day at Massachusetts Maritime Academy:

06:00	Preparing mentally for the day ahead. Normally ending with a prayer of thanks for the gift of life to see one more day.
06:30	Arrive in uniform at the office to read Bible or other leadership books. My door is always open.
07:00	Eat a light breakfast at the Mess Deck
07:15	Checking in on the student leadership team as they prepare for the daily morning parade and accountability formation. The band student leaders are warming up the band and selecting the music for the day. The honor guard leadership team is preparing the color guard and cannon teams for morning parade.
07:25	1700 students march in a parade, in formation as the band plays. The national anthem is

played by the band and the honor guard raises the American flag around the campus.

08:00 Academic day begins

09:00 Room check; a simple walk-through inspection of the student dorm rooms mainly to check-in on student general health and well-being. I love to chat briefly and see what's going on in their lives.

1000- 1200 If I'm not in staff meetings, I'm in the office with door open working on accounting, logistical support, and planning. However, my door is always open to students and I love it when they come in to talk, ask for guidance or advice. It makes my day! Even when they only come in just for me to unlock their dorm room because they misplaced their key.

1200-1230 Lunch in the Mess Deck

1230 - 1530 In my office or around campus, in meetings

1600 Academic day ends

1600 - 1700 Honor Guard and Drill Team practice (two-three days/week)

1700 - 1800 Band rehearsal two days/week

1800 Dinner

Let Them Lead

"When the student is ready the teacher will appear. When the student is truly ready... The teacher will Disappear."

- Lao Tzu

I emphasize student leadership daily. I have 30 student leaders under me helping to run the day-to-day operations of the college's oldest organization: the regimental band, honor guard and drill team, also known as "The Pride of the Regiment." Nearly all of them are juniors and seniors with a few sophomores serving as well. I rely on them heavily. Student leadership is the key to the unit's consistent success. We are the busiest student organization at the college, and one of the busiest collegiate organizations of its kind in America. On average, we perform 150 times a year in front of live audiences totaling over one million people. We travel throughout the country. We are often in Boston, New York City, Washington, D.C., and Florida. We are also frequently called to perform for the governor, whether he needs a color guard, a band or singers for formal occasions.

A lot of students graduate and go into the military, into management roles in the maritime world and every sector in between. My students are successful because they have excelled and grown in their leadership abilities while at the college. The band, honor guard and drill team organization are their training ground; a hands-on leadership simulator. They have learned to lead in the toughest environment by leading their peers, as well as all volunteers, that could quit with no recourse at a moments notice. The students work hard every day to represent the college. I believe we are doing something right because once our students graduate, and go direct commission into the military officer corps, or join the maritime officer ranks or other management and leadership jobs, the feedback is always similar, "Thank you for empowering me to lead and giving me the room to grow into my own leadership style!" They take that confidence coupled with humility and what they have learned here and successfully transition into an array of leadership opportunities.

"To thine own self be true..."

Everyone knows that I can't handle the slightest of messes or things out of place. I'm total OCD! In the mess hall, when I am eating with students or colleagues, there is a container in the center of the table with salt, pepper, mustard, and ketchup. Usually, before I get to the table, they take all of the condiments out and move them around the table just to watch me put each one back in its place.

I recall a few months into my new job, it was a very busy week for me. I did not get a chance to look in on the students on the top floor of the dormitory, better known as the 05 Deck, "The Penthouse". It was typically just that one deck that was out of order because it was upperclassmen that needed to be checked frequently to hold everyone accountable. One afternoon, I got a word from a supervisor about students in the 7th Company (Band, Honor Guard and Drill Team). The word was, "They are messy and they are leaving trash all over the place up there on deck." This all came rolling downhill because the President walked through the dorm showing it off to visiting dignitaries, and saw how bad it really was. At that time, the dorm was the newest and only in its second year of operation. He could not believe they were living like slobs! The pressure was on me to be abrasive and try to emulate a Marine Corps Drill Instructor.

I called a meeting of all the students on that deck to meet me in the study lounge. I wanted to address the whole deck about the messiness and how I was getting heat from my superiors. I walked to the front of the room and as best I could, I tried to appear angry without cussing. I told them how upset I was and embarrassed by the conditions. I was even pacing and appeared overly dramatic. After I finished, one student named Mike, stood up and said, "Sir, you know you don't have to scream and tell us this. Just tell us to clean it like you are doing." They saw right through me. They knew I was frustrated about the mess, but my delivery told everyone that I wasn't comfortable in my own skin. These young people could tell that I was not being authentic. What a relief!

As a leader, I learned firsthand to be authentic with who you are. It's too much work trying to be someone else. The funny thing is that years later Mike's wife Sara began working at the college in career services. Mike went on to get a merchant marine deck officer license and drove ships. He later went back to school for engineering and works for an engineering firm handling government contracts. Mike leads several people in his current position. He also came back to the college and gave talks on leadership.

"Where there is no relationship or connection, there can't be leadership"
- Unknown

It's interesting how when I talk to my colleagues or students about CCD, my one in one million genetic disorder, they don't get it. They say, "you're fine!" I remember when I would praise a student for doing a good job, and they were confused because they tried to read my face and my facial expression was blank. Of course, I knew how to smile, but I didn't think it was necessary. Starting out, I thought I could do a great job without building a rapport with the students. I shied away from building relationships because I thought it would make me a less effective leader. In my mind, being more transactional seemed to be the right thing to do. I was wrong.

In hindsight, the most rewarding part of my job is the relationships that I have with my students. When I see them light up when I remember something they told me about their parents or sibling, it makes me feel fulfilled. I see the fruits of my mindset adjustment when students come back to visit from several years ago just to catch up and seek my advice. I always let them know how important my time spent with them meant to me. Making a connection to impact a person's life is the key to effective leadership.

> *"... whoever wants to become great among you must be your servant."*
> *- Matthew 20:26 (NIV)*

At the end of the day, Matthew 20:26 is my mantra. It's truly how I live my life. I do everything I can to serve students to the best of my abilities. My superiors always say that I can be too accommodating. They have not grasped the satisfaction of servant leadership. If my students have to mop the floor, I will do it with them. If there is something that needs to be moved, I will move it or move it with them. Nothing is beneath me. I believe that you must be willing to serve others or the mission first before you try to pick up a microphone and lead them.

Liberty Foreshadow

Each year, we try to take the band to hear The Boston Pops Orchestra. It is still one of the most amazing orchestras I have ever heard. Every time I attend, I think about the superintendent's speech at my Liberty High School graduation ceremony. He boldly stated, "I see people in this 2003 class being Olympic gymnasts, sports stars, and even the next conductor of the Boston Pops." I was blown away because he was actually alluding that last part directly to me because I had conducted a piece the week before in the Spring band concert. It was the most exhilarating feeling of my life. At first, I was timid walking up to the podium, but when the music started I was in my zone. I got my first standing ovation! *How did he know I would end up near Boston from Ohio?*

What's even more amazing is that I can still wear the black tuxedo from JCPenny that my mother bought me to wear at the Spring concert for my conducting debut. As a young person, I never wanted to conduct. I thought it was for older people. A few months before the spring concert, a teacher handed me a baton and I took offense. I thought he was telling me that I was not good enough to be a performer. A few months earlier, a friend bought me a baton as a birthday gift, and I jokingly told him that I didn't want it. I actually felt that people were inadvertently not supporting my professional trumpet player dreams. I had a selfish attitude. I wanted to be a player and not the coach. My dream was to always be on the field. Well, look at how things turned out. I'm now on the field and on a huge ship!

CHAPTER 16

The Power of Love

Love is patient, love is kind. It does not envy,
it does not boast, it is not proud. It does not dishonor
others, it is not self-seeking, it is not
easily angered, it keeps no record of wrongs.
Love does not delight in evil but rejoices with
the truth. It always protects, always trusts,
always hopes, always perseveres.
1 Cor. 13: 4-7 (NIV)

I read an article on a research study which said that the *average* person falls in love four times in their lifetime. My first thought was, *what is average?* My second thought was, *lucky for me since I'm one in a million! Therefore, I can't be the average person they're talking about.* Ever since my date to the orchestra with the radiant Laura at 11 years old, I hadn't seriously considered dating until I was in college. But by then, I was socially awkward and proudly wore the "Mad Dog" label. I was on a mission to succeed and be the top trumpet player in the elite YSU band, the YSU Wind Ensemble. Once I didn't make the band, I set other goals which required me to stay focused on music.

A few years later I thought I found "the one." I was very much into her, yet she was very much into everything else. My mentors advised me to slow down and not open myself up because they knew I would get hurt. They were right. I spent eighteen months being in an extremely stressful relationship. I wouldn't wish my plight on anyone. After it was over, it literally took me a year to recover. Then, for the first time, the true power of love, struck like lightning.

> *"When I say goodbye it's never for long*
> *Cause I know our love still lives on*
> *It will be again exactly like it was*
> *Cause I believe in the power of love..."*
> **- Luther Vandross**

I convinced myself that there had to be some real success to online dating. Like anything else I put my mind to, I made a decision to give it my all. Then, when I least expected it, there was a profile for my one and only, "Lindsay." She was beautiful in her profile picture, with a bright, contagious smile, as she stood dwarfed in a pink summer cocktail dress by two women she embraced on either side of her. She also served in her church and was a preschool teacher. I knew I had to connect with her because she had two positives i) a woman of faith and ii) she loved helping others by working with children.

We messaged back and forth on the website. I asked if we could meet for dinner. We exchanged cell phone numbers and we texted and talked for hours. Lindsay suggested that we meet at the Museum of Fine Arts in Boston. It was the best first date I ever had! She was so comfortable to talk to. We then went to Pizzeria Uno and we both had cheeseburgers and fries. Everything about her is so genuine and kind. She also has a great sense of humor. I was truly blessed to have her by my side for my brother Lee's funeral. She helped me handle a lot of the details and made sure everything went according to plan. I honestly don't know if I would have made it through Lee's funeral and dealing with his estate issues if it were not for Lindsay's encouragement and support. I truly believe in love and Lindsay has raised the bar for me as to what love looks like and feels like. It's been nearly three years of dating and despite a few outside challenges, I look forward to making her Mrs. Magee someday. It is through those outside challenges and how we support each other in spite of them, that lets me know what we have is REAL. It is the definition of LOVE, written out in red, and lived out by Jesus himself!

"So listen up, and you will hear it
A symphony from above, it's the power of love
So glad we've found it, now there's no way around it
Just let the feeling sweep you off your feet..."
–Luther Vandross

Turn the Tide

It's no coincidence that I wrote an essay titled, *Picture of Diversity* in *Turning Tides*, the Massachusetts Maritime Academy Literature and Arts Journal. I honestly believe that we need to turn the tide and reverse our thinking as it relates to our differences. We hear the word "diversity" often and it has become a politically correct buzzword. Everyone is talking about it, but are we truly achieving it? What is missing in the picture of diversity from the U.S. narrative? I believe beautiful pictures are on display everywhere around us, but no one is paying attention. I'm not just talking about skin color. Subsequently, science has concluded that the human race is all only different shades of brown skin pigmentation, known as melanin. Even the lightest-skinned persons on Earth, albinos, still have a small amount of brown pigment in their skin. Given that, there are no black people or white people on planet Earth. We are *all* simply countless shades of brown.

When I seek diversity, I don't perceive skin color as the basis by which to clearly define our differences. Simply depicted, diversity is the nonexistence of sameness in thoughts, deeds and/or practices. I make sure that the path I take in its definition is one that may differ in thought and approach from those commonly held by many. The last thing I would want to do is to live as a photostatic copy of someone else. To have two of the same beings in thoughts or deeds means that one of the "two" is unnecessary. You will always lose resolution when you make copies. Do not be a copy, be an original. I have lived and worked with people of many ethnic groups and would say my limited experiences in and of itself does not define diversity.

Instead, diversity is living, working and creating with people who refuse to be copies. Those who are always pushing themselves and others to be their best and to see the value in others who have a different social-economic status, ideological, theological and political backgrounds, on the same team, at all levels of the workforce. This is the picture of diversity that works. Not simply finding an array of people of various melanin levels and calling it diversity. That would be like objectively calling a box of crayons an assortment of markers, pens, pencils, and paintbrushes.

Finally, diversity is not new. It started since the Creation. Humans, along with all other species were made male and female. A diversity that works is seeking out people who may look, speak or even think differently than each other, to reach a common goal, coupled with the desired betterment of the world we all share. Diversity, in essence, is demonstrating a form of love that God originally intended.

CHAPTER 17

Helping Heads
Ask for Help

*"Sometimes it takes more courage to
ask for help than to act alone"*
- Ken Petty

A sking for help often has a stigma as a sign of weakness. It takes strength and courage to ask for help. Early on, I did not see it that way. I was stuck in the stereotype of being looked upon as needy. I never wanted to be a burden to others. I had the mentality that I could do it myself - no matter what the task. Over time, I felt stressed because I was trying to do so much on my own when I was just a text message away from someone who could help me achieve a goal without much effort on their part. Once I recognized that most people have a genuine desire to help if you just ask, I changed my thinking. Then, after a person helped me, I was eager for them to recip-rocate and ask for *my* help. Turns out, I felt even more fulfilled by sharing my gifts or connections with someone else. It was a win-win.

While a freshman at YSU, at the end of each semester, you had to sit before a board, called juries. As a trumpet player, my jury was comprised of Dr. Krummel and other members of the brass faculty. I was required to play scales and perform a music selection from memory. For sophomore year, I had to play an étude from memory. An étude is an instrumental composition that is difficult, yet designed to give the musician practice in perfecting his skill. I loved the piece, however, I had trouble following the process which consisted of a computer accompanying me to play the background parts.

During my weekly trumpet seminar, Dr. Krummel would call several of us up to play the required pieces for practice in front of the whole studio with the computer accompanying us. The first person went up and had a little issue with the computer messing him up, but he faired well. Then it was my turn. I got up there and started with no problem. Then it happened! The computer somehow did not read my cue, which I had to trigger via a foot pedal. I was so thrown off and disoriented. I felt so embarrassed. Immediate fear came over me for the first time in my life playing music.

Music was, in essence, my shield from fear. Normally, once I picked up my horn, fear ran out of the room. Yet at that moment, it was like being back in grade school and the kids were picking on me and calling me "heart head" or "E.T." again. I lost my cool for the first time in my life publicly, and exclaimed, "I can't use this thing!" I ran off the stage. I was angry and felt defeated.

Later, I used that embarrassing moment to prepare for what lies ahead. My jury performance was a few weeks away. I encouraged myself and asked for help from my peers on working with the computer. I practiced with the computer every day and I entered the jury ready and confident. I passed with flying colors and earned an "A" for the semester. It was then that I started to truly comprehend that you can't do anything of value alone. That's why this T.O.U.G.H acronym is so important to me. Every word chosen was truly a lesson for myself. I had to remain **Tenacious**. I had to seek **Opportunities** outside of my comfort zone. I had to embrace **Unity** and work with my bandmates. I had to engage in every **Group** activity I could find to sharpen my skills and keep me positively focused. And last but certainly not least, I desperately needed to ask for **Help** to pass an important class.

Operating solo will only take you so far. If I hadn't realized that principle in that brief moment of losing my cool, there is no way I would have passed the class. "Mad Dog" was finally beginning to break out of his "me against the world" shell. My walls were being torn down all around me. Even *The Lone Ranger* had Tonto to help out in dire situations. *What was I thinking?* No man is an island, and for good reason.

Nose Blindness

"Ask for help not because you're weak, but because you want to remain strong."
-Les Brown

Often we go blind thinking we have all the answers and refuse or are too ashamed to ask for help. We are like those that have gone "nose blind" to our own self-reliance concept. I made a decision early on in my professional career to always seek improvement, strive for perfection and settle only for excellence in all that I set my hands to do. I knew the only way I could completely achieve this charge was by engaging others - asking for help. This is no easy feat! To ask for help is to admit dependence on another. You are opening yourself up to be vulnerable, yet this is where true growth can happen.

One of the most powerful exercises I have done is a 360-degree review. In this type of exercise, you are asking others for help in understanding your leadership effectiveness, what you can do to improve your leadership actions, and to gauge how others view you. This is a TOUGH thing to do. However, in doing this it was beneficial to my growth as a person and a leader. I sought out people I trusted from every part of my life. I asked my co-workers, my supervisors and the people I served, my students. Lastly, I asked my friends and my mentors. This process gave me a cross-section from all angles and degrees of people in my life that I knew would tell me their truth about their perception of my strengths and weakness. Here are the questions I asked of them:

(1) What are my strengths? (What do you think that I do well?)

(2) What are things you would say I'm passionate about?

(3) What are my weaknesses? (What are things/areas that I perform poorly?)

(4) If you could give me any role (job title/responsibility) in any industry or institution, what would it be and where would it be?

In doing this TOUGH exercise I found out that a key area I was doing well in was being accessible and approachable. For improvement, I was advised that I should delegate more tasks that could easily be done by others so that I could have more time to do those things that only I could do. I was blown away by the honesty I received. Please, know that when you ask for help, nine times out of ten you will get people's best attempt to come through for you. Once I received the feedback, I wrote down the responses and compared each response to others to find similarities and differences. I often found it necessary to ask clarifying questions to get a better understanding of context. Here are some of the follow-up or clarifying questions I asked:

(1) Help me understand the circumstances that lead to your response. Specifically, what do you mean by that?

(2) Can you give me an example?

(3) How do you think that I can do better next time?

Finally, it is through this exercise that I got out from under the smell of my own perception. The fog of my self-induced nose blindness was lifted and I had better clarity on how to improve. I did not take the feedback and insight as a personal attack on me but used it as a tool for my betterment. Seek authentic feedback that focuses on what you are doing, not on who you are. Don't allow yourself to become defensive and stay in a nose blind state of mind. Asking for help sets you on a path to becoming a greater version of you.

Knowledge-Sharing

"Success unshared is failure."
– John Paul DeJoria

This point cannot be overstated: everyone needs support or encouragement from another person to succeed. You cannot be an army of one. I was fortunate to have several great mentors who invested in me at a young age and continue to do so even as an adult. Seek out mentors who can help guide you through your goals. Today, mentorship is less formal, without structured meeting times and assignments. Nor does it have to be a person that is your senior. The key is finding a person who knows a task or skill that you desire to learn and just ask them questions. Sort of as if *they* are on an interview with you. Then you can share your experiences with them and begin to create this symbiotic relationship where both of you grow and learn. Even if it is not a mentor-mentee relationship, help from others can take on many different forms, like lending an ear, assisting with a chore or simply making a connection.

Don't let fear of being a burden or fear of admitting that you need help stop you from asking. It is in those times when you want to accomplish something important or make an event in your life less stressful, that asking for help will be rewarding. We all have negative voices in our heads that tell us "He's too busy to help me!" or "Why would she want to help me anyway? I'm just a student!" Muster up the courage to ask for help. We were all put on this Earth to help one another.

CHAPTER 18

Outro (Coda)

"My story was never mine, to begin with, but it belonged to all those who saw me go through life defying odds."
– Wayne Magee

In writing this book, I felt I had no choice. I believe I have experienced **Tough Blows**, not to keep this journey solely for my own remembrance, but to share with others. The T.O.U.G.H acronym has been a formula for my life - field tested and sure to be a tool for anyone to use towards their own personal success.

It took time for me to realize that I had to share this part of myself with those beyond my small suburban Ohio community. Sadly, it took the death of many of my loved ones who knew me before I really knew myself, to push me to where I am now. As you are reading these final thoughts, always remember that all things are possible when you put your faith in God.

Subsequently, this book has been a means by which I wanted to honor my family. As I write this, I am the last male alive from the "Magee" clan. I felt it was imperative that I write my journey down to honor them. My family legacy has been service to God and community. My mother, Ida the Great, impacted hundreds of families and children for over 50 years. My brother Lee, taught high school and coached sports for over 30 years. All of which left me a legacy of service to others and community above self. My goal is to carry on the family legacy by continuously living a "T.O.U.G.H." and fulfilling life by helping others reach their potential. Not only by defying the odds, but by eliminating them.

Being born with cleidocranial dysplasia (CCD), a rare genetic disorder in the medical books, I don't consider myself disabled. Despite exhibiting a few physical characteristics of CCD which include an enlarged head, lack of adult teeth or a collarbone, I have achieved my personal goals of success academically, musically and professionally, that is beyond what any medical practitioner would have viewed as possible. Sometimes as a child I wished I did not have CCD. I had my "Why me God?" moments. But after every trial, it was self-evident that God was using those situations and circumstances for my good. I want to be that reminder, that encourager to those that are challenged by their physical circumstances. Timing is everything and I believe that this is my defining moment to share my story. I have been blown away by the current visibility of CCD on full display by Gaten Matarazzo, a young actor on the hit Netflix series, *Stranger Things*, who was born with CCD. The writers of the show give viewers a real insight into CCD.

Gaten has become a celebrity champion to raise awareness of CCD and an inspiration to his peers.

Looking back on my life, I can clearly see how every well-placed **Tough Blow** led me to my path today. It is through all of the blows, the hurdles, the labels, and setbacks, that God's hand was at work. I often catch myself if negative thoughts surface in my mind like, "*I am not good nor smart enough to be where I am*". Yet I am reminded of the grace of God that showed me favor in every challenge.

He allowed me to see my purpose and to be "*Tenacious*" in the pursuit of my dreams. In all of the many "*Opportunities*" where I sought to better myself for my innate purpose, He opened doors. I learned "*Unity*" within myself first before I could be unified with others. I learned I could only do something of significance by engaging a "Group," my personal group, for guidance and to hold me accountable. It's just like my mother always said, "birds of a feather, flock together! Who you surround yourself with either becomes you or you will become them." Lastly, I learned to be humble enough to ask for "**Help**." Ill-placed pride is the killer of truly living a "T.O.U.G.H." life. There is no way I could have written these words without the many people who helped me and invested in me along my journey. So, no matter how embarrassing you may think it is, never be too proud to ask for help. By doing so, you will be one step closer to achieving your goal. Keep believing. Stay focused. Never stop working hard. Always march to the beat that makes you move deep down inside.

A Special Message...

As you have seen throughout this project, Mr. Jerry Allen has been instrumental in every aspect of my life. When he was told I was working on a book, he offered the following response below. I was not sure where to put it, but I believe allowing Mr. Allen to have the last word is more than fitting.

"I am proud that Wayne has begun to overcome his past. He has grown into a very reliable and a productive citizen. Watching Wayne set goals in everything he wants to do and then seeing him accomplish them is rewarding. He does not sit back and wait for things to happen. He keeps in rememberance where he came from. He does not look down on people. He does not reflect on his accomplishments.

Personally, my heart is being a servant and leadership is what I focus on a lot. But I found out that you don't get to pick and choose where you will serve when you are dealing with biblical perspectives for God. He puts you where He wants you to be. It was a tough decision to be with a child like Wayne and he could have died and I would have been devastated. It also showed me that I did not mind doing things that most people would not want to do. There's something deep inside of me that is always challenging to my environment. I would never just take anyone's word about something and seek to find the truth for myself. It motivated me to be with Wayne. God gave me the opportunity to speak up for a disadvantaged child and I am truly a better person for it."

Mr. Jerry Allen, Me, and Mrs. Vilma Allen

ENCORE

Awards & Letters

Never Give Up ...

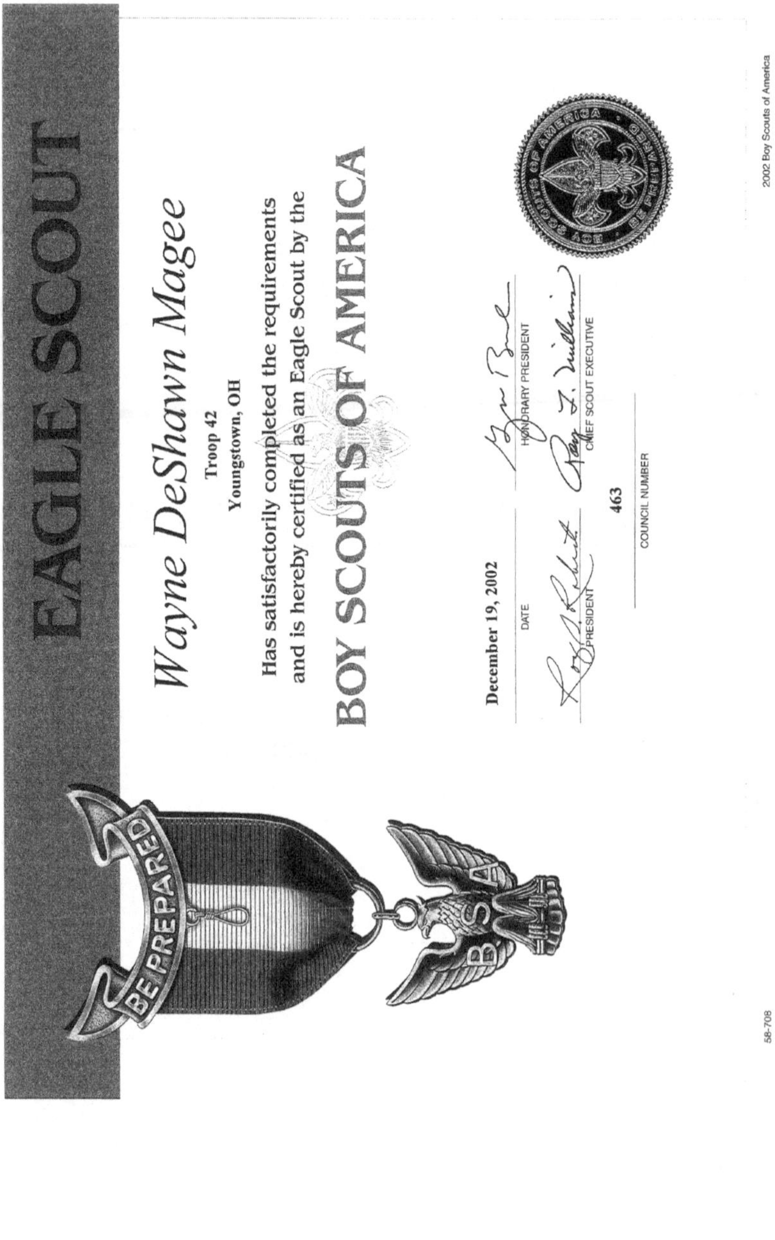

EAGLE SCOUT

Wayne DeShawn Magee

Troop 42
Youngstown, OH

Has satisfactorily completed the requirements
and is hereby certified as an Eagle Scout by the

BOY SCOUTS OF AMERICA

HONORARY PRESIDENT

CHIEF SCOUT EXECUTIVE

December 19, 2002
DATE

PRESIDENT

463
COUNCIL NUMBER

BE PREPARED

BSA

2002 Boy Scouts of America

58-708

160

Golden Clef Music Scholarship

This Certifies That

Wayne Magee

Has received the Golden Clef Music Scholarship

Awarded by

The Liberty High School Instrumental Music Department

On this 2nd Day of June 2003

Michael E. Summers Director of Bands

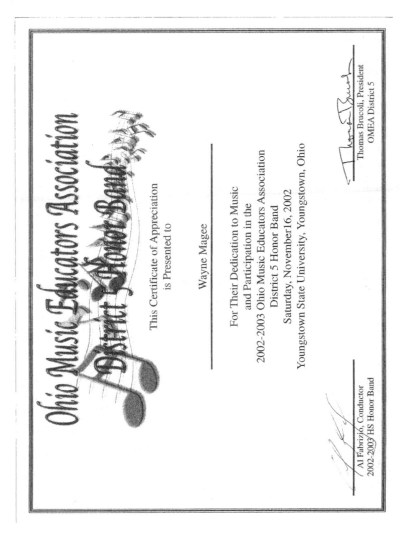

Ohio Music Educators Association
District 5 Honor Band

This Certificate of Appreciation
is Presented to

Wayne Magee

For Their Dedication to Music
and Participation in the
2002-2003 Ohio Music Educators Association
District 5 Honor Band
Saturday, November16, 2002
Youngstown State University, Youngstown, Ohio

Al Fabrizio, Conductor
2002-2003 HS Honor Band

Thomas Brucoli, President
OMEA District 5

LIBERTY HIGH SCHOOL

Awards to

Wayne Magee

Liberty Band Boosters Scholarship

William A. Rupert, Counselor

John Young, Principal

President's Education Awards Program

presented to

Wayne Magee

in recognition of

Outstanding Academic Achievement

2003

President of the United States

LIBERTY HIGH
School

Rod Paige

U.S. Secretary of Education

John Young
Principal

THE "SEMPER FIDELIS" AWARD
FOR MUSICAL EXCELLENCE

Presented to

Wayne Magee

*by the United States Marines Youth Foundation, Inc.
and the Marine Corps League
In Recognition of Diligence,
Dedication and Musical Excellence as a Performing
High School Bandsman and Soloist.*

Awarded this 2nd *day of* June, 2003

Band Director

A. M. Gray
General, U.S. Marine Corps
29th Commandant of the Marine Corps

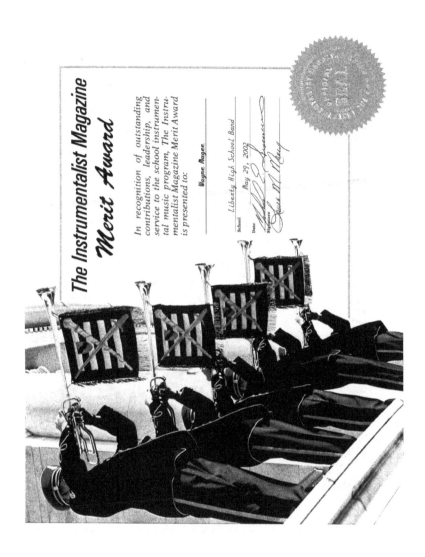

The Instrumentalist Magazine
Merit Award

In recognition of outstanding contributions, leadership, and service to the school instrumental music program, The Instrumentalist Magazine Merit Award is presented to:

Wayne Magee

School Liberty High School Band
Date May 29, 2002
Signature

Youngstown State University / One University Plaza / Youngstown, Ohio 44555-0001

March 3, 2003

Wayne Magee
625 Murray Hill Drive
Youngstown, OH 44505

Dear Wayne,

I wish to congratulate you on your recent audition at the Dana School of Music. The audition committee was impressed with your musical and academic achievements. We are pleased to accept you as a freshman at Dana. We are looking forward to having you join the Dana community and we are confident that you will find our program intensive and very rewarding.

Final decisions on Dana School of Music scholarship awards are not made until all freshman auditions are completed. We expect to decide award eligibility soon. If you qualify for a scholarship award you will be notified.

Just a reminder, if you have not applied to the University, please contact the Admissions Office at (330) 941-2000 for an application. You must be accepted by the University to be eligible for admission to freshman status and for academic or music scholarship awards. The application must be completed as soon as possible.

Please note that all music students are required to study piano for a minimum of two years during the freshman and sophomore levels. If you have had two or more years of private lessons, you may wish to audition for advanced placement in keyboard studies. Please arrange an audition with Larry Harris during the week before or the first week of classes.

We wish you every success and look forward to welcoming you in August. Please feel free to call us if there is any way we can help you before the beginning of school. Auditions for placement in the various Dana ensembles occur during the first week of school. Your applied teacher can answer any questions you might have regarding these.

Congratulations again on your excellent audition!

Sincerely,

Tedrow T. Perkins

Tedrow Perkins, Interim Director
Dana School of Music

TP/su

www.ysu.edu

169

20 June 2012

LT Wayne Magee
P.O. Box 523
Buzzards Bay, MA 02532

Dear LT Magee:

It gives me great pleasure to inform you that you have been selected as a recipient of the Massachusetts Maritime Academy Employee of the Year. As part of your recognition, you will receive $1000 and a personal parking space convenient to your office.

You were nominated by your co-workers, recommended by the Academy's selection committee, and then designated by me as someone whose contribution to Massachusetts Maritime Academy is truly outstanding. Specifically, you are recognized by this citation for representing the Academy in a most professional and honorable manner as the Director of the Regimental Band, Honor Guard and Drill Team. In over 30 events this past year, from Buzzards Bay to Washington, D.C. and covering nearly 5,000 miles overall, you have led the Band and Honor Guard to a level of professionalism and pride never before achieved.

Also, and in addition to your regular duties as a Company Officer, you served as the Morale & Welfare Officer aboard the 2012 Sea Term. Although you had never previously visited any of the ports of call, you arranged "once in a lifetime" opportunities for cadets to visit some of the best attractions that the ports had to offer, including white water rafting, horseback riding, and snorkeling, among others. These programs were cost effective, engaging and kept our students safe.

I personally congratulate you for a job well done and extend my best wishes to you in your continuing work on behalf of the Massachusetts Maritime Academy.

Congratulations and thank you,

Admiral Richard G. Gurnon
President, MMA

cc: Personnel file

One of Nine State Colleges Serving Massachusetts
101 Academy Drive • Buzzards Bay, MA 02532-3405 • Tel. (508) 830-5000 • Fax (508) 830-5088

170

ABOUT THE AUTHOR

Wayne Magee is a native north-eastern Ohioan, where he earned a Bachelor of Music degree, cum laude, from one of the nation's oldest music schools, Youngstown State University's "Dana School of Music". During his time at YSU he was privileged to perform in the University's Symphony Orchestra; America's oldest collegiate orchestra, under the baton of the late Mr. William Slocum.

Wayne later earned a Master of Science degree, in Leadership Science, from Northeastern University's "College of Professional Studies" in Boston. His music career began in working with the community youth touring field and concert band, the "Warren Junior Military Band", the band was composed of students from all over the Midwestern state's region. He later served a summer as brass and marching instructor for the Liberty High School "Golden Leopards Marching Band," a band of which he was a lead trumpeter and student conductor alumni. Wayne is a freelanced trumpeter and music educator. He performs in local bands enjoying genres from gospel, jazz, Americana, to the contemporary sounds of today. He has also served as a trumpet instructor for local public schools.

Wayne is a proud Eagle Scout and holds professional affiliations, memberships, with the National Eagle Scout Association (NESA), the College Band Directors National Association (CBDNA) and the National Band Association (NBA). Lieutenant Magee has been working in the University of Massachusetts system, serving at the Massachusetts Maritime Academy since 2008, in the Residential Life and Student Services department as the administrator in charge of the "7th Company" student dormitory complex. Wayne also has the distinct honor of being the longest-tenured director of the "Pride of the Regiment ", the Regimental Band, Honor Guard, and Drill Team along with directorship over the Student Leadership Training program.

Wayne is a passionate consultant to many, especially, in the non-profit sector where he advises leaders on developing others within their organizations, as well as, internal and external best practices on effective communications coupled with strategic planning. Wayne is also a published author, photographer, poet and essayist. He has written on topics ranging from diversity, professional career development, personal growth to personal finance.

CCD RESOURCES

We are all in this together. Below are organizations committed to helping those affected by CCD or in need of facial surgery. Visit their websites for more information on how you can help.

FACES: The National Craniofacial Association

(423) 266-1632

(800) 332-2373

P.O. Box 11082, Chattanooga, TN 37401

http://www.faces-cranio.org/Disord/CCD.htm

CCD Smiles

(707) 84SMILE

info@ccdsmiles.org

https://ccdsmiles.org/

Operation Smile

3641 Faculty Blvd.

Virginia Beach, VA 23453

1-888-OPSMILE

1-888-677-6453

1-757-321-7645

https://www.operationsmile.org/

Akron Children's Hospital (Craniofacial Center)

Considine Professional Building

215 W. Bowery St. - Suite 3300

Akron, Ohio 44308-1062

(330) 543-4970

https://www.akronchildrens.org/locations/Craniofacial-Center.html

Boston Children's Hospital (Cleft and Craniofacial Center)

300 Longwood Avenue

Boston, MA 02115

1-617-355-5209

http://www.childrenshospital.org/centers-and-services/programs/a-_-e/cleft-and-craniofacial-center

T.O.U.G.H. RESOURCES

In order to progress in your new T.O.U.G.H mindset, the following resources can provide valuable life skills information to help in your journey.

Continuing Education
Online Courses
www.coursera.org.

Career Advice and Guidance
The Ken Coleman Show
https://www.kencoleman.com/

Personal Finance
The Chris Hogan Show
https://www.chrishogan360.com/podcast/

The Dave Ramsey Show
https://www.daveramsey.com/show

Leadership and Entrepreneurship
EntreLeadership
https://www.entreleadership.com/blog/podcast

Craig Groeschel Leadership Podcast
https://www.life.church/leadershippodcast/

Life Lessons for Teens
Anthony O'Neal
https://www.anthonyoneal.com/

Public Speaking
Speaking Up Without Freaking Out: 50 techniques for confident and compelling presenting Matthew Abrahams- Kendall Hunt 2017

CONTACT

For Bookings & More Information

www.toughblows.com

46042404R00116

Made in the USA
Middletown, DE
23 May 2019